Waste Not

BY

GEORGE V. HENDERSON

*To Tanna
Best with*

THE PUBLISHER

June 17, 2004.

First Published 2000, The Publisher
Second Publication   2001

ISBN 0-9685032-2-5

CONDITIONS OF SALE

This book is dedicated to Marlene and Ken,
Lynda and Keith. Friendship is everything

THE PUBLISHER
17-7000 McLeod Rd., Suite 272
Niagara Falls , Ontario Canada
L2G 7K3

Printed in Canada by The Publisher
Niagara Falls Ontario

Waste Not

Chapter One - Tuesday 4:15 P.m.
The Cruise Ship Albianna ,The Atlantic off Cuba.

In The Beginning

I did not know the answer. I did not even know the
question to the answer. However, I knew they were
connected. The mind floats about as the wind
created by twenty-one knots cruising speed, blows
back over my resting body. I am camped out, in the
partial shade, of the great burgundy stack adorned
with spreading golden eagle wings which centered
the Empress deck.

The I of course is Michael D'Iverville McFurson
part time courier for the British Secret Service and
full time marketer.

For once I had lucked out. The Develin group of
Toronto were shooting their swimsuit catalogue and
had booked a seven day sojourn on Albianna, a
fifty-six thousand ton floating pleasure palace. The
best part was, that along with Nome, renowned
photographer , good friend and long time associate
in the real world, I am packed off with five
gorgeous models .Not to mention various body
guards, stylists and wardrobe people. Being a small
firm the hoards of boy friends and other hangers on
were not invited.

Joy! A free vacation on the high seas for myself and the wife who deserved it. Of course her mother had to come down with the plague or something. This was not totally life threatening, just enough to make my beautiful spouse stay home. I reasoned, pleaded and finally my other half said she would go. Of course there was a relapse.

So here I am alone in the Caribbean sun with limited need for my services, as Nome runs the show and eight meals a day.

A bevy of skimpily clad passengers pass by a number of whom outshone our fabulous five offering appropriate scenery.

The biggest problem for me was to define a personality for the shoot. This I was working on at the moment. Well no, I was dogging it but then no one was complaining.

Travel by ship is highly recommended. Each day offers a myriad of things to do. There was a full casino for instance. Loosing my hard earned money was never a high point on my agenda. However, during a short blow the first night out of Fort Lauderdale ,the nearly empty casino drew me in about two in the morning in a fit of insomniac dementia .My mega attack on that open door to vast fortune was placing a coin in each of the dollar slots across the back of the room. Winning and losing , at the end of the row I was forty dollars ahead.

Putting the money in my pocket I walked out. Bully for me. Most gamblers didn't leave.

The Vegas like shows presented every night are great. Offering lots of semi-naked nubile young men and women strutting their thing. First run comedians are flown out to do one night stands on the ship. In many cases this means working to the band. The band has heard it all and so if you can get them laughing you win. The guests are allowed to join in.

The dancers in their off time work in the casino, teach aerobics and run the steeple chase or other games of chance during the day. Everyone works aboard ship.

A little Scots girl gives a great massage which is on the level no hanky panky. Her powerful meading hands leave you feeling ready to whip wild cats.

I spend a lot of time looking out at the royal blue of the ocean. The sea is my place.

Once long ago, in another life, I was an officer in the Royal Canadian Navy. Memories of plowing across the Pacific on one of our arthritic destroyers to Hawaii still call me to that sequestered life. I truly believe I would have stayed a sea fairer. In for my twenty-five years, out with full pension and a life of experiences to bore people with at the old age home but things change. I met a flower child and fell in love. I now have three kids, a mortgage and a job.   If you are honest you make a decent living but that is the trade off.

For the moment I am perfectly content. I miss the wife and will be good but the scenery will keep me horny until we meet again. She had better be ready.

The wind is soft and cool, making the eighty degree heat livable. I pull the Panama Jack down over my eyes and settle in to sleep sprawled in the afternoon sun. The rumble of the ship's engines wash over me, rocking my mind to sleep, as if a babe in arms. I slide along the edge of gentle oblivion listening to Albianna's powerful heart pulling her onward toward Puerto Rico.

"Very impressive McFurson , work much?" Says Cherie-lee's satiny voice. I raise my hat slightly to gaze on a wind swept wave of crimson hair floating about astonishing blue eyes and a wide beautiful smile, attached to a body so sensually perfect that I am hard pressed for words.

" I am pondering the magnitude of the mind in search of the perfect creative direction. My dear!" I do a bad W. C. Fields.

"God, your full of shit." is the enjoinder. Cherie-Lee and I are the two eldest on the shoot. She all of thirty-two and slowly losing her form. Soon time will cause her to stay home and go into business or get pregnant. We are both married and stick together as the rest are not. They are younger and more ravishing then my tormentor.

That pack of demented fun seekers and the deviltry it causes is hard to keep up with. So we oldsters have dinner together and dance afterward, while the children as we call them tear up the ship under Nome's watchful eye. He will probably sleep with all of them before the trip is over. It is not really acceptable behavior but he is single and feels honestly he gets more out of the girls if there is an intimate connection.

"Whatever are you looking at McFurson?" Cherrie-Lee asks offhandedly.

"The blue and ageless sea, my dear." I continue a la Mr. Fields.

"You are a lech McFurson. You are looking at my exquisite body." Cherie-Lee says, contouring her lightly tanned bikinied hips for my waiting gaze.

"Is it exquisite my precious? Does it have fat around it's nasty little ankles?" I return, Cherie Lee laughs in a sweet modest way.

"Shut up, McFurson you creep. What good are you if I can't nag , haggle and control you with my beautiful body?"

" Someday Cherie-Lee, I may even teach you how to make hot dogs, if you're good. Then you will see my real worth."

" I know how to make hot dogs. What kind of an air-head do you take me for?"

" Not the way I do it," I smile a nasty sexually reptilian smile.

" Ugh, promiscuity and you a married man." She bitches playfully.

"Ugh, and you a married woman.' I counter.' So are we on for dinner." I change the subject.

"Yeah! Sure. They have a new comedian and he is supposed to be really good. Ella knows him from New York." Ella is the German girl with the wheat blond hair and small bum. She spends her free time learning English so she can make it in the movies. No one questions that she is a spectacular model. However, as an actor my fat, furry, old dog could do better, faking starvation to cadge scraps from the table. So what other Nordic actors have made it, why not Ella?

" Mike."

"Yes."

" Rinny wants you to go to see her about the set this afternoon. She thinks Nome is shooting her with too much profile. She won't tell him, of course,

cause he's such a monster artist.' Cherie-Lee
shrugged, 'she wants you to tell him."

"I don't think so. Nome needs me to give him
advise like Gomorra needed a pimp." I shake my
head. Getting involved with petty feuds between the
shoot components is sure death. Neutrality is the
only way.

"Well you better tell her. She was crying." Cherie
made a face like she would like to give Rinny a
good kick.

Randy Tinny was a brunet, small and cute. She
had the kind of smile men lust for, with a nasty bit
of challenge in it and a compact body to back it up.
Randy Tinny was also a nymphomaniac or as close
as you get to it. There were few men who hadn't
had her. I and the Pope seemed to be the only
exceptions. . However, she was a seasoned veteran
at nineteen and maybe she was right? Anyway I
would tell her no, best to nip these things in the bud.

" Where is she?'

"In her cabin I think?"

" You come too." I demand.

"What, you need a chaperone?"

"With that one I may need a crow bar."

Cruise ships are two-thirds stairs. This is to allow
the guests to work off all the food they've

scarfed down. Below decks we walk on thirty ounce blood red carpets past brightly decorated wall murals to the Athens deck. All our cabins are situated here in a block purchase. We stop at cabin 345, which is sea side and mid ship. I knock, while Cherie-Lee wanders down the corridor to look at the acropolis just up the way.

"Yes." says Rinny's voice with a giggle. If I had any smarts at all, I would have twigged but Cherie - Lee is my friend. The fink!

"It's Mike McFurson Randy." I say hoping for some reason she is indisposed. The door opens slightly.

"Come in." Rinny says, vaguely from behind the door.

I push it open and step in. The door slams and they are on me. Misty and Laura both take an arm and press their nude bodies against me holding me against the door. Rinny tries to pull my trunks down before whipping around to get the camera I spy on the table behind her.

It must be said that having three women, models at that, doing their best to be close to you is a unique and pleasant experience. The smell of perfume and the feel of bare flesh is overwhelming.

Misty is almost albino, her eyes are even slightly pink, her skin is alabaster, her hair snow white. She normally does cover work but is doing a favour for Nome on this shoot. At twenty her body is full and perfect. She has a slightly haughty look which works well. Now, of course, she is giggling like a school girl, trying to give me a hickey to maximize the potential embarrassment. The photo, which I presume will be held over my head, is to get everything they want and more. It is the more that scares me. Nothing like that kind of photography showing up at the house.

Laura on the other hand is all of seventeen. She is stronger then her thin body looks with steely muscles under her deceivingly thin arms and legs. She has that kind of a starved look, accented by honey blond hair and blue bell coloured eyes. Laura has great legs and just enough body to go with her full breasts . She shaves her mons, I notice and looks like a four year old, which I find a cold turnoff. Misty wears black silk see through panties. Other than that everyone is nude.

Now you know this isn't going to happen.. I hug all the girls together catching Rinny in the middle of the squirming flanks and begin to tickle.

"Don't I'll pee!" Misty whines and falls in a heap on the floor. Laura puts up more of a fight but finally collapses laughing on Misty who howls her anger. Rinny jams her fingers into my sides and scores points until I turn her around, smack her hard on her tight little behind and propel her onto the pile. She screams at the indignity, as I grab the camera from the table and get their picture sprawled there on the floor. Presented is a wondrous collection of legs, breasts and bums, Rinny's being predominant.

I put the camera down as the chorus of angry female voices rises in volume. I smile down at them.

"Children!" I taunt as I make my exit. Just in time to hear things hitting the closed door behind me. Cherie-Lee stands open mouthed at my escape. .I glare at her and she holds her hands up over her head to perfect herself from my wrath. I would never hit a woman well, only where they sit. As I pass her on the way to my cabin I left hand her beautifully rounded behind . The flat of my palm impacts with crack that closely resemble a rifle shot. I am rewarded with a yelp from my crimson haired victim and saunter down to my cabin.

Chapter two - 5:10 P.M. Athens Deck, The
Albianna

Making Hot Dogs.

My cabin is large and bright with a light blue
motif. In the corner is a glass lamp which is an
Athenian shield. The bulbs behind it create a golden
light when it is lit. There are two single beds that
can be put together to form a queen size sleeping
place. Compact buff coloured cabinets and drawers
are cleverly inset into the wall by the door. The
bathroom is directly to your left as you enter on soft,
blue carpet. The thing I like most about this cozy
little fortress is the porthole or more realistically the
window, that provides the heavenly light streaming
into this comfortable place. The steward, a pleasant
spoken Jamaican named Mondi, has been at work.
My clothing is folded and the bed is immaculate. It
is nice to be pampered.

Shoulda, woulda, coulda rings in my mind. Don't
get me wrong, my baser dynamics told me to charge
in on my 'would-be' attackers and hump their little
behinds until I have a coronary or something fell

off. However, skinny models really didn't turn me on. Also the whole thing was just to get me for not accepting Rinny's high power 'come on' ten minutes after we got on board. Under normal circumstances she wouldn't have taken the time to dump wet dung on me. However, she hadn't had me before, and well she should, shouldn't she?

Misty, I ruminate, might have been alright alone and clear of drugs, which she took although no one and everyone knew.

Then of course there were the standard reasons why not. AIDS, someone screaming rape, pregnancy, being hauled out by the body guards and placed in the brig. Oh yes! I was married.

Question, was it just a harmless prank or did the assailants mean me some harm? I, of course, had short info sheets on everyone including the luscious Cherie-Lee from London. None of them had any political leanings unless it was the choice of booze or cocaine. No, I was being overly picky. The majority of models I knew were nice clean kids who were involved in an adult world at a very sensitive age and required to swim with the sharks. The sharks were very nasty.

I did not feel they were really out to get me.
However, I did have my twig. This was the internal
alarm bell that dictated I was being followed. It was
a sense developed from over 15 years with the Firm.
Who would represent a potential danger on this
ship? I should be reasonably worry free. I wasn't on
company business and who would know I was here?
The cast of characters on board the ship were, mobs
of boomers , a lot of young lovers and single, older
women looking for a convenient mate for a few
days. The normal revelers with the money to enjoy a
five star floating hotel. It was better a number of
years before competition increased and the rates
dropped. Then a better class of people shared the
ships. The current group tended to be more chintzy
less apt to give tips which were required at the end
of the week of fun and sun. The service had suffered
in direct proportion, as the crew members got
almost nothing in salary and the tips provided their
living.

You now had the good tippers, who got a lot of
service, the maybe's who got less and the tentative
who were lucky to get clean glasses.

I had seen no one who looked like they might be a
problem. I would send a report in to the Cleveland

cutoff through Brit line on the internet and obtain a guest list just to see what we had.

I removed my trunks and did the three cleansing breaths of yoga. This insured that my body would empty of inner evils. I do a little yoga daily but I can't stand on my head anymore.

Having loosened up I did a karate cotta, with emphasis on the kicks and punches as well as blocks. I don't do a lot of hand to hand fighting but you never know when it will be called for.

I was bugging myself and gave up the exercise for the shower, which is another challenge . You take time on a ship getting the shower just right as the hot water comes directly from the boilers. You don't want your lily-white skin boiled off.

As to the toilets, there are legends of small children being sucked ass backward down the crapper given the tremendous gurgling wild beast suction . You had better count all your equipment when you get up.

I, of course, am kidding. The shower is excellent and I feel much better having gotten four gallons of suntan lotion off. My body had not completely gone to seed. I had been lifting weights. The old gut looked pretty good. I slapped the hardened surface of my belly . My butt was heavy, but solid, I can't seem to

get that down but it wasn't terrible. Who am I
kidding? I'm fifty. The thought depressed me. I
guess being healthy, doing something I loved and
having those who loved me, should make me feel
better. The problem is, you can see yourself in the
mirror and you know. I still had most of my hair. It
was only getting a little gray. I had the urge to
colour it but hell, well, not yet. Got all my teeth.
Jesus, this is really depressing.

A horrible thought came to mind. What had I left
behind? What had I done with half a century? Well,
three kids, good ones, not on drugs or booze. I
won't speak for sex but at least no one was
pregnant.

I had marketed for companies all around the
world. Changed some opinions, moved a lot of
merchandise. Most people don't realize that
seventy-five percent of the stuff we use in the west,
we don't need. Guys like me talk you into it. I was
good at what I did and I didn't lie to my customers
or their target segments.

Oh yes! I saved the world. Well most of Chicago
anyway (see Covet Not). I was the richest man in
the world for about ten minutes (see Spy Not).

My work helped keep the world safe for fifteen years. The information I carried as a courier allowed Britannia to rule it's ever shrinking empire. Once in a while I become a line agent with predictable results. No one would ever know what I had done or seen. Maybe some next century scholars will look in the old files and see my name. Maybe they will be impressed, maybe not. You see, I am a Canadian.

The Queen still rules in Canada and I gave her my word, so I kept it. I will not knowingly do anything to harm the country of my birth and work outside it, for the most part. I gave my wife my word too and kept it. Well, I sinned once but not again. Cherie-Lee is right, I am full of it. At least I passed up a real opportunity with the models today and I was good. Chalk up the brownie points.

At this juncture in my pondering there was a tentative knock at the door.

"Who goes there? " I snapped off.

"It's me." Said a small voice.

"Go away Cherie-lee. I am not playing with you anymore, you Quisling." I intimate high dungeon. It is fake and she knows it.

" Come on it was just a joke." She whines.

"You're full of it Cherie-Lee, it was a premeditated attack and I'm working out my assault report right now." I tease through the door but laugh a little at the end.

"Listen McFurson do you want to eat alone or what?" She teases back.

"Ok, come in but if the pack are with you you're permanently off my Christmas list."

"I open door and step back quick just in case. Cherie-lee is alone, leaning against the door jam, clad only in her green bikini. She enters and walks over to the nearest bed to sit.

Placing her elbows on her knees, she cups her round face in her hands. I find this appealing as it is little girl like and very her.

"You really mad?" she asks a little afraid I might be.

"No." I shake my head to the negative and sit on the edge of the dresser.

" What's a Quisling?" she asks and I feel older than God.

"When the Nazis were in Norway, he ran it. He was a turn coat."

"Oh!" She says, not really interested. Under normal circumstances, I would not be alone in a

room with a woman, dressed only in a towel.
However, Cherie-Lee and I went back ten years.
We have always been friends.

Although I've never had one, if I was to have a
sister she would be Cherie-Lee. Not that she wasn't
of interest. Under a shoulder length crimson fall, of
silky coiffure, was a large forehead and magnificent
sea, blue eyes that shone out on a room guileless
and pure. The nose was a little small, I thought, for
her face but it gave Cherie a kind of every woman
look that her full sensuous mouth empowered, with
a wealth of shared joy. You at once wanted to be
married to, be having sex with or just sit in a quiet
room watching the rain holding Cherie-Lee.

Her neck was elegantly refined and white. The
slightly tanned shoulders supported two full breasts.
These were real, not implants like Misty's. An
hourglass extended down to full hips and long
exquisite legs. At the moment her right foot covered
her left. If Cherie-Lee had a fault it was her feet,
which were huge. Most models have this problem.
However, what would you expect, the woman was
at least five foot ten or better. I was only a little
taller then her in bare feet. Cherie was kind enough
to wear flats so we balanced out on the dance floor.

Models were always hiding their feet. Normally these apendages are shot straight on or partially hidden to compensate.

Cherie -Lee is beautiful beyond words and I enjoy just looking at her.

All of a sudden tears begin to well in the bottom of her eyes and drip down her face. Fingers rush to cover up but she sobs.

"What's the matter?" Perfect, that was brilliant.

"Don is sleeping with someone else." Cherie-Lee says looking away. The pain is obvious.

" How do you know?"

" Rinny told me. The little bitch. He's sleeping with Claudia." I knew Claudia, she was twenty-two and French with that elegant Parisian flare. My crimson haired companion's husband Don is an international stock broker and a nice guy or at least he seemed to be.

"Rinny, I wouldn't believe her on a bet." I started.

" I know it's true. I suppose I didn't want to believe it. Rinny just put a name on it. She was mad, thought I told you about the little party they set up." She wiped her eyes smearing her make up in the attempt.

"It almost worked. I tickled them, dumped them on the floor and took a picture with Rinny's bum right in the center.' Cherie-Lee laughed then and I thought we were over the rough part.

"I guess I shouldn't be telling you should I?' She sniffed 'you've got your own problems."

"Come here." I pulled her up and hugged her. She didn't stop me. We trusted each other that much. The tears came then and flowed for a good few minutes. The scent of Channel filled my nostrils and her soft body had its effect. I moved away a little to give room for my esteemed person to grow. She didn't seem to care or ignored it, staying close, clinging to me, like someone on a precipice.

Women at a certain age know they will deteriorate. Their bodies will not maintain a youthful form. They hate themselves and as a result, take it out on anyone in the area. A lot of hassled husbands can't take it but I knew that wasn't the case here. Finally, she stopped crying.

Why would anyone cheat on Cherie-Lee? Interesting question. Checked out your own glass house lately?

Cherie-Lee sniffed and wiped her nose with the back of her hand. The make up base came off and a myriad of freckles appeared. I smile.

"Now you know my secret McFurson. I'll have to kill you." She tried to provide a smile but it was lost in more tears.

"Come on Cherie-Lee you don't know for sure."
She did, of course and her broad honest face started
to show signs of anger.

"He's done it before but this time she's really
young and I'm really old. I can't fight back Mike
I'm falling apart." If you're falling apart, I'd like to
fall just here too, I thought but didn't say it.

"You are spectacular and if your husband is that
stupid he needs his head examined." I say it
truthfully but feel terrible because I have broken my
vow. It was only once, still I cannot escape the
realty. I see my wife's face in my mind's eye and it
destroys me. Cherie-Lee's face becomes very intent
for a moment.

"Mike do you want to have sex?" she asks cold
and to the point. She wants to get even. How do you
answer that one? What do you say? Would I? Yes!
My mind screams Run! Run! Run!

"Like I said, someday I'll show you how to make
hot dogs.' I joke and turn away to the tray
supporting a bottle of Seagram's VO , a variety of
soft drinks, some ice and glasses neatly set. 'You
want a drink?" There I changed the subject. That's a
start. I hear the soft rustling but figure she has
seated herself on the bed.

I turn with the whisky in my hand. Cherie-Lee was naked.

If you could bottle the vision of sexual potential, I was seeing, no living male on the planet would ever need those little blue pills again. She was facing away to offer her behind. Slightly bent at the waist with her fine hands on her thighs, beautiful blue eyes twinkling come hither over her left shoulder. Her full beasts tipped with candy pink nipples moved softly, pert and firm. I had never seen Cherie's bum before, I mean completely. It was, and I can say with some authority, the absolute best, period. Her cheeks formed a perfect heart, being slightly saddled, rounded as opposed to squarish at the hip and perfectly proportioned.

"You were going to show me how to make hot dogs right?" She said. It was more of a plea then a statement. If I closed her down hard, as I should, she would be destroyed and I couldn't do that. To hand her a rejection when she had come to me for help would be inexcusable. So I removed the towel and moved up behind her. I placed one hand on Cherie's soft full right buttock, the other came to rest on her left shoulder and with one motion I straightened her. She gasped.

"What are you doing ? Is this going to be kinky?" her voice was shrill. Cherie was stretched like an elastic band.

"Yeah, of little faith." I snorted, while reaching down and separating her perfect nether cheeks slightly, then lay my aroused body between them.

"See ' I said as she looked back frightened over her shoulder.' A wiener between two buns is always a hot dog." It took her only a second to get the joke. Her laughter was like a popped Champaign cork, the tension and fear bubbled out. Cherie turned and brought one hand up to her mouth.

"That is the cutest thing I've ever seen. That is so cute." She giggled

"You must have done that when you were a kid?" I smiled shyly.

"You did that with little girls. God you're a pervert

"Actually I was a prevert, being all of eleven at the time." She laughed again shaking her head.

Then she hugged me. Lord I will admit I put my hands on her perfect behind but then I pushed her gently away and put the towel back on. At first Cherie looked a little hurt.

"I guess we aren't going to do it, are we?"

"Its not that I don't want to, you can see that." I smiled and she nodded and smiled back.

"Look we're friends. If we make love we will be something else. I kind of like us this way You just went through a big hit. You need to look at things and see where you want to go.

Having sex with you would be the best thing I could ever have but it would break the meniscus and we would never be the same. Maybe it never will be again, Don't hate me. If I did I would be taking advantage." I trailed off knowing I had screwed it up. Strangely enough friendship is able to understand if it is real.

"Well at least you can still get it up McFurson " she teased as she covered her perfect body. 'And,' her voice dropped slightly, 'It 's beautiful too."

"Thank you.' I said . What the hell else do you say? I can honestly state I have very seldom blushed in my life but I could feel the crimson fire of it cross my cheeks.

"If you need me I'll be just down the hall' she said with a wink, then more quietly 'Thanks for being my friend." With that she left.

Chapter-Three -5:20 P.m. - The Albianna Cabin
349, The Athens Deck

A Shove In The Dark

I sat for a moment after Cherie - Lee left and
considered the reality of what had just happened. I
wasn't uncomfortable about it. I had done the right
thing. Perhaps that was important. I would regret
not taking advantage of the situation later, like all
men. On the other hand my friendship, which had
been nurtured over many years would remain. Of
course if anyone made hot dogs with the wife, I
would do what ? Kill them of course.

I was appalled to find my mind asking the question
what was the bet between Cherie and Rinny over
who could get to me first. However, I dismissed it
immediately.

Perhaps Cherie-Lee was a blind side, another one.
For a spy, one is deadly. Time to start being a
member of the Firm again. Time to find out what
was exciting my internal nervous system, telling me
that I had unwanted company.

Tapping away at the lap top, I asked the Firm
through Brit Line on the internet for Albianna's

passenger list. I also included some marginal information to Theodore (Granny) Boothby-Staters the head of the North American Section of the British Secret Service about the situation.

Having done everything I could at that moment. I lay down nude to sleep until dinner. In the soft silence of the room I looked at the situation more objectively.

The girls trying to embarrass me by debagging my esteemed self, was surprisingly, quiet normal for the end of the millenium. Sexual barriers were disappearing. The young were trying things much earlier. By the time they reached maturity there was no right of passage just a gleaming eye on the watch for even more radical behavior and sexual enjoyment.

My eldest son tells me of two teenage girls who, while on a sleep over crept into the hostess's elder brother's room and shaved his legs while he slept. It was funny but not something that would have happen in the past, before the liberation of women and the decline of moral values.

In another case, a young lad was sexually involved with a girl. She in turn invited her girl friend. There was a menage a trois which lasted until the boy left and the two young ladies carried on nicely, thank you very much. These were high school students.

The new rage, I had read somewhere, was that couples were using strap on sexual devices. This allowed the girl to mount her boy friend ,husband et al. It was depressing. Cherri-Lee's damaged marriage was another indicator of the fall.

Perhaps the root problem was the loss of controls on personal enjoyment, the responsibilities that went with sexual and other freedoms that no one seemed to want to know about.

What had happened to men? Where was John Wayne when you needed him? Men were questers who had been bamboozled into believing they were second class women . What kind of man would allow some girl to put on an imitation organ and jam it where the sun didn't shine?

Men had climbed the highest mountains, explored the deepest jungles, followed rivers to their sources and walked to the poles. We had been to the outer edge and would be again. Soon man would go into far space. I believe freedom would call on mans need to see the next horizon to go out where no one had gone before. For riches, fame or just to see what was beyond the next planet.

Not unlike the Vikings in their open long ships braving the North Atlantic with only a sail and the strength of their backs. We will venture out to face the unknown in starships this time, as the hunting pack, we have been since we dropped down from the trees. At least I hoped it would be that way.

My gender, I was taught, consisted of gentlemen. A man spoke his words and lived by them. His clasped hand was a deal that was followed to an equitable conclusion . A man held his drink. He worked hard and was esteemed for his work. A man paid his debts and treated women with respect. He spoke to other men and was treated as an equal. Now every man is defined by the media, in a destructive frenzy, as an animal who raped and abused women or had sex with his children. This was the mantra even when only a few percent were involved in these hideous crimes. More often in the media, he was an idiot who was regulated to degenerative duties. A buffoon for the amusement of his offspring.

The respect for heroes was gone and we have none for our boys to look up to. Young men are committing suicide in greater numbers because they feel alienated, confused and deceived.

It was time for men to work at promoting themselves going fishing ,going to the game, telling their boys of real heroes. Not the feminized pansies that towed the P/C line, but real men . Sir Edmund Hillary , Terry Fox and Harry Truman. Strong durable competent men who faced the future with the trust that it offered. Men our sons can emulate. New adventure still calls these young men as of old. The depths of the ocean and the vastness of space were the next vistas. Tell them they are not evil from birth, just normal. It was this thought that McFurson went to sleep on.

My Epsylon woke me at exactly 5:45 with time to dress for the captain's invitation cocktail. I had purchased a tux for the trip. Sid Silver was having a sell off of older units. My purchase was fine, with limited wear and no shiny parts. I suit myself in front of the mirror just getting the tie squared off, before I am to pick up Cherie-Lee .I didn't look too bad. The bedroom brown eyes gazed back with insight . My high cheek bones provided a lean wolfish persona.

The list of the ship's company was E-Mailed in code along with a nasty pointed question as to what I was up to, excellent question. The group looked pretty normal until I got to the Viscount Suites. Senator James Tilly jumped off the page. The senator was a known bag man for his party and a big friend of the current American President. What would he be doing on a lower end cruise line?. Maybe the trip was free but well it was something to look into.

Finally after looking over the remainder of the list without finding much else. I walked down the red carpet past other revelers to the humble abode of Cherie-Lee . I knocked and she was ready . Cherie-Lee is perhaps the only female alive who can be ready on time and look like she was about to do a Vogue cover.

Her exquisite body was draped in a Lincoln Green, velvet dress. This attached behind her neck and flowed down over her breasts clinging to the front of her form while providing magnificent cleavage.

"Tada!" she smiled that wonderful smile she blesses her close friends with.

"You, of course, as always, are ravishing beyond words ." I bowed.

"You don't look too shabby either." She returned the compliment.

"No , I'm beautiful." I corrected and she laughed
and blushed, in equal parts.

The Captain was Italian, a common situation on
these ships. For the most part the newer sea palaces
are built in Italy. He was a distinguished man in his
forties . The broad aristocratic face exploded into a
smile at Cherie-Lee's approach. He made love to
her hand and looked at me with unbridled envy,
little did he know. Other passengers wait in line
while he exchanges pleasantries and Cherie graces
him with her charm. By accident while watching I
complete my mission for the shoot. We will use the
fine nautical silhouettes of the Albianna's officers in
uniform as a frame for the girls. I make a note to
discuss this with Nome but I am sure he will
approve.

We sweep in and drink free martinis. The brats
show up. Rinny is unforgiving but Misty apologizes
and Laura giggles. We all start and can't stop. Nome
of course has the picture of the girls in a pile
processed. Rinny is furious, especially when I
mention, I seem to have caught her best side but in
the end she too laughs a little.

Cherie-Lee whispers she isn't wearing any
underwear. I must say I am a little shocked but lift

the material over her bum just to check.

"McFurson, you creep." she scolds and jabs me hard in the ribs while blushing furiously. She is telling the truth.

Entering a room with Cherie-Lee on your arm is like making an Oscar walk. Waiters in the main dinning room fall over themselves to see that things are just right. Cruise cuisine is five star. As we peruse the leather bound menus, I watch the crowd to see if anything shows up on my warning screen.

Nome appears from nowhere and slides in next to Cherie-Lee who protests but makes room. Prentice 'Nome' Hallerin is short, perhaps five three but is built like a weight lifter. Blond hair is coifed back from his face, which is cliche movie star. He has a strong forehead, flashing, blue eyes, a straight nose and a full house of capped teeth, set above a dimpled chin. The arms are powerful but subtle extending to fine fingers. Nome also sports a barrel chest sliding into a powerful lower torso and legs. For all of this Nome tends to be caring of people ,has a unique way with the models and most important he has the eye. It is not the camera or the lens that makes the picture. It is the eye. The vision to see the photo before it happens or as it happens.

To see the components and make sure they mesh.
Nome was a master. The sun had to be at such and
such an angle. You wait three hours, in mindless
boredom, then in three seconds it's over and the
image is perfect.

"What have you two been up to? " He asks in a
surprisingly deep voice and a look that reeks of
sexual innuendo.

"Nothing!" I am the gentleman and tell the truth.

" Rinny says different."

" She's just mad I got her bum for posterity."

" God that is awful." says Cherie -Lee laughing.

" I don't know' says Nome pointedly, 'should you
guy's be carousing in McFurson's cabin?"

" We always carouse in my cabin. The main deck
tends to be crowded." I snap back but Cherie-Lee
looks wooden and uncomfortable. Nome sees and
looks at me and says nothing more.

" I hear Senator Tilly is on board." I change the
subject before Cherie spills her guts and it gets
messy.

" Yeah, that's him over there with the army."
Nome nods.

The good senator is seated with an attractive dark
haired girl who looks vaguely Chinese but perhaps

not. He is also surrounded by four CIA types, which is interesting as his security should be from the home state. I wonder why?

The center of attraction is handsome in a Midwest sort of way. He looks like a high school football star who has gone bad. A large, clean face. A smile that carries a certain amount of conceit. Intense brown eyes and a body positioning that signaled intense concentration which are learned and phony. Unfortunately it probably worked real well back home. His body had put on pounds over the years. The Senator was slightly tanned wearing a white dinner jacket. His dark hair was beautifully combed and had no sign of gray, although he had to have at least five years on me

The girl was beautiful and elegantly fragile in a soft sensuous way. Her small hands moved like butterflies but only occasionally. The girl's eyes were brown and lustrous. Her features were fine. A cascade of black hair rivered down her shoulders. She did have an incredibly sensual mouth, which was full and always slightly open as if ready to kiss. The senator's words were golden and she drank them up like honeyed wine. She had concubine written all over her. Oh well to each his own.

The four men who watched him from every angle
with small hearing aides in their ears looked like the
real thing. Three white one black all wearing dark
suits and immaculately presented.

" Those stiffs are so intense they probably have to
take Prozac to go to the can.' Nome said and we
laughed. ' He's got more in the cabin next to his."

"What the hell is he expecting Black Beard?' I
quipped.

"I don't know but everyone is very edgy. While
we were shooting up there with "E", they stood
around out in the hall." Said Nome with a knowing
look.

" Let's eat. I expect all the attention at this table,
not some flabby Senator." bitches Cherie-Lee
playfully.

" Shall we leave Nome?" I smile nastily.

"Of course Mike " We both get up.

"You guys are rotten." Cherie huffs.

"See you later." The photographer laughs and leaves.

"Nome!" I call him back. He leans over to listen
and I describe the layout. He nods and makes some
comments. I know he will think about it tonight and
have lots of ideas for tomorrow.

Dinner is spectacular. It being Italian night we start
with anti pasta and then go to Veal Parmesan which

is light and excellent. I order Blue Parrot, a German
wine. I have always liked Mosel vintages. The food
goes down with stories and an endless gossip which
Cherie prides herself on. Her little known facts
about the fashion community are always fun and I
laughed a great deal.

I bypass the desert tray for orange sherbet with
Cherie-Lee who is always watching her weight. The
meal is satisfying and the show afterwards is
wonderful. Half of the ship's guests herd into the
Empress Theater, which takes up two decks at the
bow of the ship. The other half go into the later
serving.

After the show I and my crimson haired
companion, dance in a variety of the discos and
finally end up in the 'Aft Deck' a dark piano bar.
Where we waltz and laugh in the soft darkness until
almost eleven.

The night air is fresh and sweet. Cherie and I
walk along the deck together, stopping along the rail
to watch the moon, which is almost full. Behind us
the band in the Aft deck plays a slow seventies tune
which I can't put a name to. I am full and happy.

The night has been excellent and Cherie-Lee makes
me feel important and loved in a friends way.

" Well what would you like to do now? " She asks
holding my arm tightly.

"I would like time to stop now I guess. I don't
think I could feel any better. Tomorrow will be the
same hopefully but soon we will have to go back."
That was a stupid thing to say. Cherie tightened up
and let go of my forearm leaning on the rail.

"Tell me McFurson what would you do in my
place?"

" I don't know. I would sure find out about Don
before I took any action. Then well, its up to you.'
Sorry, I just can't go on Rinny's nasty little shot. If
you're sure then I guess confrontation and all the
end results or you can ignore it and go on. The
problem is if he is running then he'll continue to do
it. The question is how much can you take. If it's a
one time thing well then you have to weigh it." I
paused because I had had a one time thing and I
knew how much I hated myself for it.' I am the
worst one to ask. I really don't know."

"Thank you for that completely indecisive and
very male answer." She kidded and I laughed.

"Well if you don't want my highly priced non

advise why did you ask?" I said smiling.

"I'm getting cold,' she said, 'I think I'll go back to my cabin and take this dress off. Want to watch?" She asked.

"Cherie." I said in exasperation.

"Only kidding,' she said kindly and kissed my cheek. 'You're either the best friend a girl ever had or dumb as a post." and went off down the deck.

Well dummy what do you say? Nothing as usual. I would like to but no. Or maybe? My mind turned it over pro and con for a few minutes but I knew I wasn't going to break my word again. Although you never say never, I guess?

Strong hands grabbed my legs at the ankle and at my elbow. I was lifted up and over the railing, my hands pawed for the wood but too late. I shoot out into space. Down, falling into the darkness, seeing the ship passing, the white sheen from her wake clearly visible in the pure moon light. Down with out a net, down. I hear a scream and know its me. Water, there would be water below but we were talking five stories. Christ would my body stand the impact? I line out put my hands in front of me and try to take

a divers point so that I don't cannonball in and get
crushed like a bug. For a moment I remember that
this large metal object sliding passed at twenty one
knots has two huge propellers providing power. If I
survive the landing, then can I get far away enough
to escape the blades and their suction? My life
begins to pass before my eyes.

BANG!

I land on something solid. The pain is terrific. It
takes me a moment to realize I am laid out along a
rail. My arms and legs hang down on either side like
a dazed sloth. The pain is unique. I have never had
every part of my anatomy scream at once. My brain
tells me I am lucky I was not one more foot to the
left, the impact would have exploded my heart.
My foot is entangled in some kind of rigging. That
is what is holding me and saves my life. I get the
distinct feeling my sexual apparatus are now
sticking out of the other side of my body. I go
numb like a wounded bird, shock is coming on. I
fight it.

Alright where am I? On a painter's scaffold, that is
the only answer. It is solid and I will survive. My
mind seems to be pleased with that reality.
Question, no which side of the scaffold am I? I take
my pen out with some effort after my wind comes
back

and it takes a minute I throw it to my right. There is a slight noise as it hits the floor of the scaffolding. I heave my body over the rail to the protected surface. Sitting unsteadily in great pain, I pop one high blood pressure pill out of its aluminum holder and force it down. The two aspirins I carry at all times follow.

I massage my arm, which seems to be dislocated but the fingers are still working, so no. My tux is ruined but I am alive.

I thank God. Why he keeps me around surprises even me.

A moment later a flash light beam shines on me. In the halo of the torch I see what has been bothering me over the last two days, Toad, the last of Jewel Dubois's eunuchs . This servant of Dubois, the master pimp and ex-firm traitor, whose death I had the pleasure of watching in New Orleans, had some how found me. It had been he who had thrown me overboard. Lord for a gun at this point.

I hear the fat pimply face bellow its rage that I was still breathing over the roar of the moving ship. The light disapears, then I feel the ropes that hold the cage to its davits begin to move . It takes a moment for me to realize the he is cutting through them. I

feel the belt under me and realize its a safety line.
This I put on with some difficulty. Just in time,
however, as the rope on the right side parts and that
end of the cage swings free. Being attached I stay
with the cage holding on for dear life. I yell for help
but the words are taken away in the wind. The cage
shakes as he starts on the other side. I am for the
moment in suspended animation, then free fall, this
time with the cage attached. I brace myself as the
water receives me and my transport. Down! Down!
Down. The dark closes around me. My lungs burn
with the need to draw breath which does not exist.
In the moon light I see the propeller fin in silhouette
as it cleaves down to finish me. Then an explosion
of bubbles and to the surface like a cork. I breath in
fresh air jaggedly and bob on the seas face. The air
buoyancy, safety equipment attached to the
underside of the cage opens into an orange safety
raft. This is triggered by the depth and saves me.
The cages weight and shape has placed me slightly
behind the great turning blades of the propeller. I sit
in my small floating oasis as the water runs out. The
sea rocks me like a leaf, the dark surrounds and the
aloneness sets in. I watch the brightly lit Albianna
plow on to Puerto Rico only three hours away.

Chapter Four-8:21 A.m. San Juan, Puerto Rico, The
Street of Golden Light.

May Old Acquaintance, Not Be Forgot

The Street Of Golden Light is little more than an
alley between two thin thorough fares, Luna and
Sol. Between the sun and the moon it shines out in
pastel elegance. The island, as the locals call it, is an
isthmus, which holds the fortress of El Moro and
the oldest aspects of San Juan.

I stand in front of the three story building that
dates from before the Americans captured the island
from its original Spanish owners. The wrought iron
grill work, speaks of long ago, when Spain ruled a
vast empire and other nations slunk along for the
scraps of her wealth.

I had arrived in San Juan an hour before Albianna
by US Coast Guard helicopter to El Boqueron Base
rather than the La Puntilla Station.

How, you might well ask? It was all rather simple.
The Epsylon watch I wear has a powerful micro
transmitter. The seaman on duty at the Boqueron
radar facility must have thought a nuclear aircraft
carrier was sinking off the coast. The blip would
have dimmed just about anything else. Twenty-five

minutes after I turned it on the patrol copter screamed into view. A line was dropped and I was lifted aboard in great pain but with nothing really broken. The Coast Guard crew finding someone who had fallen off a major cruise ship complete with tux were impressed. The fact that I had survived was one for bar stories for years. There were, however, a lot of questions about the signal transmitted.

I of course simply told them it must be from the cage. This was also hauled in. There was some consternation later when no transmitter was found on the paint scaffold. A telephone call to the right parties got me released and a lid placed on the whole incident. The local CIA did ask to speak to me later. I of course disappeared into the city trading my tux for something less flashy. I moved around until I was sure I wasn't being followed. I took one of the Paradas, the small yellow tour buses that transport newcomers to different parts of the old section of San Juan. I stick to public transport for two reasons; One, it is hard as hell to tail. Secondly, with 350 violent car jackings in Puerto Rico each year, driving on one's own is stupid. The Island is also very well patrolled by the local police mounted on small jeeps dressed in green shirts and beige Stetsons. Suffer the tourist as little as possible.

I chugged along to the Castillio San Felipe Del Morro and walk around the powerful fortifications, a statement of Spanish might, built in 1571. From the ramparts hidden in one of the old covered sentry boxes, which smells fusty of old concrete, I watch my Albianna come in through new binoculars. Having purchased a cell phone, I called in to Albianna after the first passengers had disembarked. I do this to ask if the cabin steward had found my watch which I felt I had lost . Could he check out the cabin? I would be back after some sight seeing. This would cause the ship's crew to think I was still on the ship the night before.

The phone call also would allow me back on board, as I still had my boarding pass. That pimpled moron was going to jail. However, first I had to set up a little surprise, for my fat gormless friend.

The question, of course, was how did he know I would be on that ship? The answer might be at the head of the stairs I now mounted. The landing was old but clean . The smell of toast floated out into the hallway making my mouth water. I knocked.

The young man who opened the door might have been twenty but not much more. He was obviously homosexual. I asked for Jerry Reading and got an nasty jealous look.

"What ju want him for?" Asked the occupant hand on hip. The thin face was controlled by its cheek bones, which were high and angular. He was Hispanic and there was a certain personal pride in the strong jaw and the full mouth. The eyes were soft and doe like but at the moment there was a lot of anger there.

"Who is it Megel?" Jerry's soft English voice carried past the boy to me.

"Mike McFurson , Jerry." I said smiling at the guardian. He didn't smile back.

"Come in, dear boy." Jerry appeared, his thin form covered with a pink woman's kimono. Pastel flowers ran rampant. Jerry smiled with his whole face. There was nothing put on with Reading. You got what you saw.

" The sun is especially hot today.' I recite the first part of the required daily phrase.

"We will need shade I suspect." Jerry said in return.

" If it doesn't rain." I finished the phrase and moved into a comfortable garret.

"Oh, one of those,' said Megel 'Ju want me to go shopping for a while?" he asked Jerry.

"Yes sweeting if you wouldn't mind." The older

man touched Megel's hand and he left with a smile to me. My turn not to smile back. I was uncomfortable as hell and it showed.

"I really don't like people coming to the house without an invitation." Jerry came to the point. His face was thin, almost oblong. A full head of silver white hair, might have made him distinguished, if it wasn't for the robe. His long forehead dropped down to painfully light brows and two gentle blue eyes. A line straight nose brought you to a thinish mouth, that pouted when it wasn't working and a pointed but weak chin. Your standard fag right? Wrong! Jerry was a long term line agent as cold blooded as you might want. The brain behind the mask was diamond sharp and working as you watched. I would trust Jerry as I might Breakleaf, under most circumstances but today I had a problem and it had to be rectified.

" I got thrown off a ship." I say to garner the reaction.

"A ship?' he said incredulous, 'did you insult the chef personally?" He quipped.

"No ! Jerry were you out here when the slaughter happened around the time of the Bay of pigs.?"

"That's a leading question.' he said a little off guard. He paused ' May one ask why its important?" Well, the seven men who died in 1963 seemed to be tied to this but I wasn't telling him how.

"Were you?" I demanded.

"No I came out in seventy - three.' he said and moved over to the table. Why did I know there was a gun somewhere near by?

" One of Jewel Dubois' people, a fat, pimpled, git called Toad tossed me over the side."

" Au! How did he know you were on the ship?" asked Jerry.

"They told you I was on the cruise right,' I started . 'I had to input even if I'm not on firm business."

"Yes, of course!. Margaret would have been told too. " Margaret was the other active line agent in Puerto Rico. She can't be more then thirty-four. So she had nothing to do with '63".

" Breakleaf, Harry was in England back then,' I counted off the people who would be informed as I passed through the ships itinerary. Harry breakleaf was the line agent in the British Virgins and an old friend but you didn't leave anyone out. 'Henry Say of course in St. Martin.' Henry had saved my life as well as Yatomi's when I was after Dubois and Wellington in the Bahamas." I finished.

"Wellington is mid thirties. Say was here as you

know. He was damn near killed." Jerry evaluated
the list.

"How did he almost leave this veil of tears Jerry?"
"What ,Oh I believe he was shot in the chest."

"Is there anyway someone in headquarters would
find out?" I probed

"Doubt it very much.' Jerry wondered over to the
window. Between the buildings you could see the
harbor, busy with traffic. 'Its all numbers at head
office. Almost impossible to make out that sort of
message. Something like157 will be in 257 at 988
inform 688 whatever. The numbers change without
warning and often" Jerry ruminated for a moment.
'It is possible they found out in Miami. Dubois had
a house there you know."

"We left from Lauderdale." I throw in.

"Same difference, I'm afraid. Florida is honey
combed with leaks of one kind or another. War on
drugs what a running, bloody joke.' Jerry almost
snarled, ' Everyone is being paid. They don't want
to legalize marijuana even for the poor bastards
dying of cancer. Its a fifty billion dollar business
fighting drugs. Jobs, equipment sales, payoffs,
you'll see that shut down over a lot of dead bodies.
I'm afraid anyone can get just about any information
they want." Jerry trailed off.

"I wasn't scheduled to come down until two days before the ship left. The cabins were purchased en mass. I came down with a blank ticket. No one could know I was coming." That made Jerry look up.

"I see!".

"This thing stinks, Jerry."

"You should have been looking, dear boy." Jerry smiled meanly and put on his senior man cap.

.. " No question, Jerry." I admitted 'but this is now."

"True!' Jerry conceded. 'Might one know how you got here.?

"You know that buoy signal they put into the new watches, it works."

"Really, good show, the last one damned nearly got me killed. By the way you weren't followed?"

"No I took care.' I wasn't insulted, the question was valid. 'I'll need a gun."

"Will you now?" Jerry smiled thinly knowing it would come from him. Reading went to a Chinese red lacquer chest and removed a plastic box you might carry an electric drill in. He opened the gray cover and removed a Luger, 9mm Parabellum Marinen-Pistole. It was a 1904 melt with a ten shell clip and grip safety. The weapon was one of few that have survived distribution to the German Navy prior to World War One. It was exactly 10.5 inches in length and weighted about 2.5 pounds. Jerry's slender hands offered me the weapon and the thin silencer that went with it. It too would be exactly 10.5 inches. The combination would create a weapon that could be fired without even a cough . It would be light, accurate, silent and very deadly with lots of stopping power. I thanked Jerry, who grunted, he would want it back.

"What is the plan then?" He asked.

"Well, I'll inform Granny of what I have here. Lay on Harry to meet the ship in Road Town BVI, when we dock there tomorrow morning. Then we'll haul the pimpled bastard down to the local jail and ask him a few pointed questions."

"We'll go with you . I know people in Low places at the cruise line and I do Audrey Hepburn rather well,' Jerry smiled. 'I fill in for different acts that can't make it.. Megel will come along. We can back you up "

"And get a free sea voyage." I throw in.

"Folly the thought 'said Jerry his nose in the air, 'The Pimple has to have help and you are not a line agent.' He finished and started with a new set of questions. 'Anyone on board that excites the interest?"

" There is one Senator Tilly, the rest of the list looks pretty clean."

"Tilly, on that cruise line?" Jerry made a face.

"Well maybe it's a freebee. He had a Sino-European girl friend that looked like she melted with every word.' I raised an eyebrow. ' I figure he's enjoying the trip."

" I'm sure Mrs. Tilly would be pleased. I happen to know she is a rather aristocratic blond.' Jerry said softly, looking out at the harbour. You could see Albianna tied up down the shore in a new enlarged Callemarina docking facility that could accommodate nine large liners. I realized that this was an expensive little apartment, which, of course, offered a view of the harbour for a purpose.

"Terrific view." I comment.

"All the better to see what I have to" Jerry played along.

"Were there any other Chinese around?" Jerry lead again.

" No not so you'd notice. Mainly white Anglo Saxon types. The crew is a different deal as you know." I passed over the list. He thanked me and began to scan it.

" I guess there's a lot of negative thinking with the Vieques Island thing going down." I said to make conversation.

" Yes, they've voted to throw the American Navy out and with good cause. That bombing range is just plain dangerous. However , I don't think it will effect the long term interaction with the US.

" Who do you think gave your fat friend his information?" Reading asked the sixty-four thousand dollar question.

" I don't know, the possibility he just got lucky is out beyond the realm but it is possible.
On the other hand it seems an inside job, which means that everyone out here is in danger."

"You were in England before Jewel came out here did you know him in a biblical manner.?"

"You mean, did we have sex ducky." Jerry looked at me with cold disdain. Then when I thought I wasn't going to get an answer.

"Yes, I knew him. In those days it wasn't as open. Both of us were on the same team. He never asked me to give him information or told anyone at headquarters . I told Granny myself . You might be surprised to know I have a wife and two children. One's a barrister now.

"When I came out, It wasn't vanguard then. I'm afraid. Granny and Oswald his predecessor decided to use me here. There are a lot of gays here, quite a community . Very machismo if you get my drift and talkative. Mind you I was more attractive back then. The freedom was wonderful though.

"Your wife." ·

"Oh she wasn't upset. She simply found someone else. The boy still writes. The girl's married with little ones. I suspect I should see them but well duty and all that lather. I don't hear from her.' he finished sadly. 'You must find me repugnant?" He said.

" We all have our stories, just different players'. I hesitated. 'Would Jewel lie about something he didn't do? I mean take credit for something someone might have pulled off?"

" No. I mean he might if it were good for the service and so on but personally he was very honest. Mind you that was then."

' What do you see in men?" I asked thinking back to all Jerry had lost by coming out.

He turned and looked at me strangely

" What do you mean?"

"Well a woman has curves, there's softness, the fullness of her body, the small of her back, the gentle little things she does, the joy of the act. I never could find anything attractive about the male body. We're all muscle, there's nothing soft about us."

"Oh please stop before I throw up." He said a little

miffed. "Ducky, you may be the last straight man on earth." He said laughing meanly 'the things you find unattractive draw me to beautiful young men like Megel. Does what I do unnerve you so much.?"

"No! You're an agent and a good one. Hell you can sleep with sheep if you like. As long as you come through for me when I need you and I can do the same for you, then we're square. I'll be honest, with all this AIDS goin down I think your nuts but that's your call."

"And you find the act filthy and redundant." Reading probed

"A little and tremendously painful if my limited brush with proctology is any definition of the situation." Jerry smiled.

"You're interesting McFurson. I very seldom have friendships with men. It's usually one thing or complete negative. You I class a friend."
"Having a blind side can get you killed I warned." Pleased with the compliment but uncommitted.

"Yes and discussing blind sides what about Cherie- Lee and the other models anyone with the shoot that would set you up?"

"Hell no, Cherie left just before it happened but I don't think so or maybe I should.' God I hated my profession. ' No! I don't think so!"

"Find out." That was an order and I didn't like it but Jerry was right and I agreed.

"Finally of course, what if our fat friend decides to leave the ship here in San Juan. Ducky?"
"I don't think he will. He's too stupid. He's told what to do. He might, so far he hasn't left."

"How do you know?" Jerry came down hard.

"I watched the ship come in and the passenger flow. Nothing. He may be leaving as we speak. But I called about five minutes ago to ask if Turpin would need a renta car. He was still on board then. His real name is Edward Turpin, just for the record."

"Good I'll have Megel keep a watch on him."

"There is something I'd like to discuss with you. Something I want someone else to know about." Reading was worked up to the topic. That wasn't normal given everything, Jerry was reasonably decisive. I didn't like secrets. I either shouldn't know them or they could get me killed and well it wasn't my side of the business.
"You tell Granny." I asked.

"Yes, in part but not all of it for a number of reasons." He paused and seemed to grip the thin robe around him more tightly. The clouds moved to cover the sun making the room darker, as if evil was called at the speaking of it's name.

"Have you ever seen one of these?" Jerry fished something golden out of his pocket and dropped it into my hand.

The ring was unique. The gold was very old yet, only a little warn. A chain was linked through the circle. The chain was eighteen carat and newer, the ring could be a thousand years old. It was comprised of three cords intertwined with a snake's head hidden in its middle, a Latin phrase was carved inside. I was a poor Latin scholar as any of my frazzled high school teachers will witness but I could make this out.

"Vengers of the ring "I said to Jerry.

"Avengers of the ring , Dear boy." Jerry corrected.

"I've never seen anything like it, its Asian isn't it?"

"No, its Western European but it was influenced in the east." Jerry sat down and began his story.

" I knew a doctor Balboa, he was of Portuguese

extraction but has been an island resident for many years. We had mutual interests and he had some very interesting clients. That aside,. a man came to him with chest pains. He died in the doctor's office. No fowl play just death by heart attack. Completely normal.

On examining the man it was found that he didn't exist. At least not under the name he gave. The good doctor knows my interest in the arcane and gave me the ring as there seemed to be no heirs or anyone to collect it.

" I in turn put the dead man's finger prints through interpole at Granny's behest. The man is a German, Wolf Stranger , ex of the West German air force. Post war of course. He was in his forties. He was a senior technician and left with a clean record, at least when they demobbed him..

I looked around using the keys Stranger was carrying and found his apartment. It was under a different name from the one given the doctor.

He ran a small computerized design firm for various international aircraft manufacturers. Made very good money at it. I also know the odd bank manager. No pun intended" Reading smiled it was contagious. 'He had substantial funds. That means substantial in excess of six figures. I don't know what these fellows make but the amounts in his accounts here are astronomical. The IRS, where I also have some friends, didn't make the figures balance and confiscated the money."

Interesting things started to happen then. Balboa died suddenly in a car accident. It looked very clean but given what I had found out it had to be suspect. I went on the internet and began to fish around. I checked all the European libraries and found nothing. I then called up the Library of Congress and surprise. The Avengers of the Ring, exists in book form.

A fellow by the name of Joshawa Brient was the second son of the Duke of Dundern. He fancied himself a bit of a writer and had an interest in the old man of the mountains."

"You mean the assassins with the flame knives that murdered kings and princes around the Middle East during the crusades. Didn't they take a crack at Saladin?"

"Very good Dear boy." They also black mailed other people of note to stay alive, when they weren't praging good citizens for substantial amounts of money. The old bastard controlled the entire area. Had kings cringing before him until a local power, it may have been Saladin, cleaned out his little nest of vipers."

" So this an the extension of that." I indicated the ring.

"No, this is home grown in Europe. You see Brient's original book was comprised of stories of similar shady groups. The Knights Templars and so on. There was a small chapter on our friends. It was printed in Paris where he lived at that time.

A knight, Jean Mordur De Savingay returned from the crusades to find his cattle and lands in the hands of a large rival family. They had been taken over during his absence for back taxes. This, of course, was a big no, no with regards to those who had fought for God's cause. However, the villains knew the king rather well and power politics has been with us for a long time.

Jean was not amused. He couldn't take direct action so the story goes but he could find someone who would. No Robin Hood, our Jean, he found some trusty discreet fellows and surprise the entire family of the usurper died. By accident of course but dead all the same. Jean got his land back .

On the other hand, he realized there was a market for that sort of thing. Based on his knowledge of the Old Man, he decided to develop a more sinister and better organized operation. Initially it was to help crusaders who had been bilked out of their goods. The actions taken were very selective. The amount of ten percent of the property obtained went to Jean and the Avengers in gold.

The Avengers were chosen for their skills as killers. Also for what knowledge they possessed of new technology., education and so on. The number was never more then twenty, although that might have changed. There was only one knight, however, thereby maintaining the class system. When it came to the payoffs, the shares were equal with maybe a little more going to the knight. Each man wore a ring on a chain, under his clothing, to remind him he was a member and to make sure one of his own didn't plant him. The gold the rings were made of came from the Holy lands and was therefor blessed. The Avengers, of course, were avenging wrongs.

Everyone got very rich. Those who retired passed the ring on but were part of the organization until death.

The next thing you know, they have become part of the financial elite in Europe. Quietly they terrorized selective individuals. Those who had skeletons in the closet at first but later anyone who stood in the way. They still murdered, of course, but the amounts are very large and the situations very intricate. They in affect, at least back in 1874 when the book was written, controlled a substantial part of the power structure of Europe. One must suppose they have done so since the crusades." Jerry stopped for breath.

"The Boys must have been ecstatic when this book came out." I quipped.

"Overjoyed, Mr. Brient had a coach and four run him down in the high street one spring day. His death was instantaneous. There was a nasty fire at the publishers and almost all the volumes were destroyed along with the owner. Those that got to the shops were purchased en mass. Brient made the fatal mistake of sending the books to his relatives. A number them had accidents. The French police kept the case open . There is some information in the files although, many of them were destroyed. It seems just before he died a cousin of Brient's a Selmon Artien sent his copy to a second cousin in the United States. George Metre was a tin smith. He took the book and disappeared into the American west. It seems he changed his name to Willis and became quite a lawyer and later a judge in Washington State. At the end of his life the book with his other documents were sent to the Library of Congress by his family for posterity.

"I'll be damned."

"I do hope not." said Jerry with a smile and continued.

"It also seems our friend Stranger had an interest in New York. He's been up there six times, in the last six months. On four occasions jet aircraft have crashed within a day of his arrival."

" Do you think there is a connection?' Sorry stupid question."

"No! you're right. We don't know for sure but that is the point." Jerry 's face became darker. 'A few days after Balboa's death a gentleman showed up looking for friends of the good doctor. He was given some names, not mine. Surprisingly people started having accidents."

" He's looking for the ring?" I asked

" He is looking for me." Jerry said." I put out the word and the accidents stopped."

" I'd have Granny send out someone from T-section and have the bastard's ticket punched." I said furious.

" Of course you would." Jerry passed over my reaction as it reflected my stupidity. He would need to follow up. It was also a matter of professional pride that he not be scared off. Anyway the man's death would have simply caused him to be replaced. In turn the planes if they were the result of his influence, would continue to drop.

"What are you going to do?" I asked sheepishly.

" The man, a Swiss this time, Jean Monblanc is also an aviation specialist." Jerry continues. 'He will leave here in seven days for New York."

"You intend to follow him?" I said.

" Yes, well, not officially. Its not really my area and of course, its not a British question."

"If one Brit or even a Canadian was on those flights its our business. Hell forget that. If one person is being killed its our business.

"At this point everyone thinks they are accidents and we've been told so by the US government." said Reading meaningfully.

"Which means they don't know and don't want us involved.. Screw them."

"An interesting concept, however, there is the little matter of their investigation. We might endanger that and cause a possible panic if we fowl the nest. In fairness it might just be accidental."

" So, I am being given this information why?"

" Michael, if I and Megel fall victim to an accident would you mind taking a trip up to New York?" Jerry asked politely, as if he were requesting I pick up milk from the corner store. Of course, I would go, if I was still around. The policeman in me would not let it go. Jerry knew that.

" You want me to keep the ring?" I asked.

"Yes! It will confuse them.' Jerry smiled his thanks. 'Here is a picture of the Monblanc."

Absentmindedly I placed my little finger through the ring.

"No!" Jerry yelled as he slapped my hand away. I don't like being touched, being slapped is down right unacceptable. The look on my face must have shown it.

"Steady on!" said Jerry in apology. He took the ring from me and rolled a piece of paper. Reading then inserted it into the ring. As it immerged out the other side there was a trail of brown coloured stain. I breathed out and shook my head.

" Poison right?" I said

"Absolutely dear Boy enough to kill an elephant."
He said showing me the two small razor sharp fangs
hidden in the center of the ring.

Chapter-five - 8:50 Am, MS Albianna , San Juan,
Puerto Rico.

A Waltz In The Dark.

   The night hid my return. Security on ships like
Albianna has improved somewhat. I think though,
you could get a real elephant aboard, if you said it
was a gift for someone. Retail sales is the one big
push on the islands. My black metal pachyderm
seated in the pool, spraying himself, sounded
hollow but wasn't.
   On a previous stop over at San Juan, I and the wife
were amazed when on our Shopping Flamenco
Show Tour, all the buses from six visiting ships
arrived at a single jewelry shop. The passengers
with money falling from their pockets, roared in and
bought everything in sight. I and the wife waited to
be taken to a second location. Here we could have a
little choice and purchased our small gifts at a
greatly reduced price. This does not make me
smarter I just have friends in many places.

Tonight, I am waved aboard and take the elevator to the Athens deck. I hesitated at my cabin door wondering what, or worse who, might be inside. The door opened with a soft click. I entered the darkened room inhaling deeply to catch my own scent. Something our ancestors have done from time immemorial. It insures that it is your place and that there are no intruders or have been. The room smelled neutral. Closing the drapes I turn on the light and look around. A real pro has gone over the cabin. Nothing is amiss. Someone who knows all the tricks has worked here. Not a courier though, we know different ones. Baby powder, strings and odd hairs are out. Scanners, both heat and invisible touch powder are in. He wore gloves. Why am I surprised? There are no finger prints and it was done sometime ago because the heat signature is light. I look down at the pocket calculator computer, I acquired this from Jerry, it defines all this information. I wonder if it might be a good time for Scotty to beam me up.

Toad didn't do this job in a million years, which means its a line agent. Who? One of ours?

No time for this. First, I have to make contact with Jerry who is down the hall.

I let myself out and wander down the corridor, hoping I won't see Cherie-Lee or anyone else. I knock the prescribed number of times in sequence and am let in by Megel. He is resplendent in a steward's uniform and holds a Walther.

"Ju like it? " He whirls to show off and Jerry laughs.

"Sit down, dear boy." Jerry directs me to a chair before a mini monitoring sight. Two small television-type monitors, perhaps five inches across are wired to something that vaguely looks like a VCR. At the moment the screens are still. A very expensive cabin is shown in one mini-TV. On the other is the Toad. He is laid out on the a bed of the smaller cabin, happily sleeping off a good dinner, by the looks of the piles of plates. His fat face looks boyish in sleep but I have seen it under different circumstances.

"Nice picture quality." I comment.

"It does offer something, doesn't it? It's part ours, part Japanese. We tend to feed off each other in these things. I think you'll like this." Jerry rewound the picture of the large room to a point where I could see our Senator friend and his paramour. He was dressed.casual but chic in Hilfinger. She was naked. Her honey coloured body statued beside the bed. Her clothes, which were nicely set out were very expensive. She is Chinese. I am sure of it. Her pert little breasts offer themselves extended by thinish brown nipples. She has no behind to speak of. The legs are nice, however, I whistle. Jerry snorts and fast forwards.

A thin man with glasses appears, who reminds me of a standard CPA. He receives instructions from the elder statesman. Four hulking body guards stand in a semi circle.

On the Senator's departure with his lady, the accountant gives an order handing, the senior guard a brightly colored post card. He then follows his master to dinner. This is about three hours ago I calculate. There is no sound.

"The chap in the glasses is Jeffrey's, Tilly's secretary. He just asked the troglodytes to exchange the card for an object which is to be checked before acceptance.' said Jerry as an aside. I am impressed he can read lips. 'At that point I requested Megel go down and get the same post card from the ship's store if possible." Jerry continued.

"Those guys are CIA. They should have twigged to the camera in five seconds. They must have scanned the room?"

"They're not CIA, ducky.' Jerry says cold bloodedly, 'they're just well built security guards. Yummy true but made up to look like CIA. Which, makes me think Langley isn't supposed to know or doesn't want us to think they know."

"Our security types, scanned when they went in, that was that. Megel served dinner and planted the wireless camera." I look around and realize we are viewing the target room from the center of the shield lamp in the corner.

"Cute." I exclaim.

'It gets better' Jerry manipulates the rewind buttons as if he was in a BBC recording studio.

We see a single security type move to the door. Guns are drawn the men spread themselves around the room. If they aren't CIA, they are well trained by someone.

There seems to be a certain lack of trust toward the caller at the door. Two men enter. They look

Caucasian but something makes me think they are oriental. They are short and their mannerisms give them away. They don't have guns but one holds a large metal suitcase.

Visitor One says something. The senior security type wags a finger. It seems the caller must show what he has first. There is a momentary hesitation. Then Visitor One places the suitcase on the table and opens it. I whistle one more time. You don't get to see a million brightly colored Cayman dollars all in one place too often.

"Is that a million?" I ask Jerry.

" I believe so." said Jerry softly as if he might be heard.

"That's one and a quarter million dollars US." I breath out. Security One steps forward and begins to count. It takes time, no one moves. In the end he is satisfied. Security One pulls out the post card and hands it over. Visitor One examines the card minutely, satisfied he places it in the inside pocket of his suit. The two visitors back to the door and leave. The security don't move until they are sure its OK! The suitcase is removed and the room clears.

" What's on the card I wonder?" I say

"Excellent question.' Jerry chips in., 'however, it has nothing to do with your problem."

" Meaning? " I asked

" What we just witnessed was an exchange of money for information. The two chaps with the suitcase are probably Chinese. They could be Taiwanese but I doubt it given the current direction of American policy."

"Of course, the Cayman money can be placed right into a island bank then removed after it's been suitably laundered." I added.

"Exactly, better than donations from penny poor Buddhist monks. Some idiot seems to think that providing the Red Chinese with suitable weaponry for suitable financial return will create a new cold war. As a result the Americans will suck it up and go back to depending on the fearless leadership of the minority. They have the power and of course big business who comes out best in these sort of things.

No more nasty questions about health care or if the bugger who wants to be President has any policies to speak of or can actually think. Simply say yes sir and shut up, don't question or you're a commie. You'd think these twits would twig to the fact that Vietnam did away with anything near that kind of kowtowing. The Americans will never put up with that. They're starting third parties and the power boys are scared to death. With two parties and no real choice you can control the flow of power. Three or four parties means a real opposition with a voice. You can control the press but then there is Mr. Ventura he won because he was honest. The hacks on both sides were sodded and it looked bloody good on them." .Jerry finished.

"So its the Imperial USA, Hmm."

"God knows.' Said Jerry ' let us hope not for all our sakes. Where they can vote in a known liar and then find him not guilty for a crime, which he admitted. He went on television lied to the entire country was caught at it, vented his soul and was forgiven. A hundred years ago they would have lynched him, now for his successors anything is possible." That was a somber and flawless evaluation of the situation.

"Question,' I started, ' what's on the micro dots or whatever on the card?"

"Keys, dear boy, the keys to the kingdom. More precisely the vault . Pass codes to computer terminals with clear definitions. That means there won't be any way to stop the perpetrator when they cut into the terminal. The possessor of the chip can lift, say, computer technology to direct rockets. You can't have the thermo nuclear device they already sold the East, not given proper directions to its target somewhere in little town USA. The most frightening thing is, it's all for money, dear boy. Talk about shooting yourself in the head." Jerry was in a grim mood.

"However' , he brightened, 'this time they won't be able to. Megel bumped into the oriental gentleman in the corridor." Jerry held up the post card.

"That is really great. Jerry you're brilliant." I say honestly.

"I was sure you'd notice eventually." He said modestly.

"Remember, a swelled head does not a good spy make."

"Remember, out here ducky, I am your superior."

"Sod you. Pardon don't sod you. In keeping with the situation." I kid.

"You must have taken English at the same place you learned about sex.' Said the elder spy.

"When are you out of here?" I asked

" We're changing cabins now. Whoever wants you dead has nothing to do with this. This bunch might kill you if you went right at them but they want privacy too much to do anything else." Reading said firmly.

9:45 The main dinning room Albianna

Albianna slowly moved out of port. Long streams of wake slid out from her bow. El Moro was left behind in the Caribbean night.

If Tilly and Co. were not the ones who had thrown me over board then who? I decided to have supper and ruminate.

The second seating people are almost finished their meals. Many have already left for the show. Had it not been for that, I would never have seen Sasha. As it was, there was only one reasonably full table. Eight people sat having coffee as the remains of a lavish meal was removed by the ship's staff.

Sasha Borinski was ex-KGB. You heard different

stories although the maxim was no one ever really left the KGB, even with the fall of the Evil Empire. I scanned the room. Of course, there was Legev, his bald head nodding in agreement with a rather fat woman next to him.

Russian spies went in twos like nuns. It seemed they left their firms in twos and continued their careers as a matched set. The muscular, square faced Legev would do the killing. Sasha, the rapier thin, clothes horse was equally lethal but provided the brains.

Sasha was showing great interest in a rather tweedy man seated beside him. Interesting, let's see what happens. I move to one of the two empty chairs at the table set for ten.

"Mind if I join you? I seem to have missed my sitting."

"Sure!" says a Boston accent, coming from a solidly built man in his forties to my right. His pleasantly blond wife smiles. Others join in to the affirmative. On board ship everyone is friendly. It's too good an experience to waste on negative vibes.

The waiter comes. I apologize, telling him I was sightseeing and almost missed the boat. He smiles from behind a South American mask. However, he agrees to bring steak, which will be well done with mashed potatoes and the veggie of the day.

The conversation includes me now. I am asked about the city. I comment on various sights sounding touristie. Sasha's cold face smiles sarcastically. We've met once before in Paris on one of a few trips out of my zone of operations. He and Legev are pointed out to me by the local man. They didn't see us. This was after the fall. They were involved in industrial secrets and were a French problem. This does not mean he doesn't know me.

The steak is delicious. The meat is soft and goes down well. I eat as the table clears out. The Englishman next to Sasha, is talking to two rather attractive woman. Not young but well built and panting for fun. I find out they are sisters from the US and are without their husbands. I wonder if they are looking to be bad?

The tweedy gent is one Dr. Julius Pope. He is an Englishman from the midlands. Keeping surgery in a small town in the hinterland to escape London. This also provided a better cover for other things he says sagely.

Is this guy saying he's with the firm enclaire? Hell, no one is that stupid. Spy Book page one, rule one. Never tell anyone ,anything about yourself unless it's vetted, secure and then watch out. Sasha does not recognize me or does not let on. It doesn't take a brain surgeon to figure out he's here for Tilly and his post card or is it more for the money or both? If so, my passing would not be overly grieved and Legev was certainly capable of tossing me overboard. However, they would have nothing to do with the Pimple. He was too weak a dupe and could be a liability.

The situation got curiouser and curiouser. My ruminations are stopped by the conversation which almost makes me choke on my supper.

"Did you ever have to kill anyone Juli." Asks Verna, sister one with an Ohio twang wide eyed . She is terrified but sexually stimulated.

"Well that would be telling wouldn't it." says Pope his long horse's face set in a 'Well I know but you really shouldn't' look." Good Lord! My mind tilts. Sasha grins evilly. His thin saber face is set with sly corn flower blue eyes a short blunt nose and a wide mouth. On a woman the mouth would be sensual but placed here it reminds me of the orifice of Jaba the Hut.

"I was once shot at by bandits." He says off handedly

"Gosh!" says Vera, sister two. Both women have round faces with large 'Betty Boop' brown eyes.

Vera shows more age they are late thirties and have maintained their bodies to some degree.

I look Pope in the eye. He's a cold liar. He never killed anyone in his life, or is an exceptionally good actor. I don't think so, I've seen too many.

I ask about being a doctor in England after nationalized medicine. In doing so I also drop in the first line of the phrase of the day. If Pope is real he will drop the second line or as here if he cannot respond because of the situation with Sasha he will drop a two word stopper. I will in turn leave it alone.

Instead he harumphs about the British medical system and misses the lead completely. He is no spy or at least not one of ours.

Sasha knows this too. He is about to have some fun with the fantasy super agent. Perhaps it will serve him right. My fear is that if he thinks the man is with me, then there could be trouble but I think not. If the boys had tried to throw me overboard then the reaction would have been different. Sasha is a good actor but not perfect or at least I hope so.

Sasha takes off on a tale that would shame the Arabian knights. He tells of working for the Coca Cola company fighting syrup over the Afghani hills and all over the southern part of Russia. Sales to the Moslems are good because their religion forbids alcohol . However, they attempt to steal his product. The two open mouthed women are shepherded over burning deserts, through sand storms, camel shortages, gun battles and dark deals with various evil characters. At one point Sasha who has crept into a local chieftain's tent, to sleep with his voluptuous daughter, becomes so specific as to make the entire group pant. The Russian tells how in the end the two lovers are forced to bite down hard on leather straps, so that the screams of pleasure, created by their love making do not wake the sleeping poppa. This minor error would cause their instant demise. The crowd is mesmerized. I believe the two sisters actually weather orgasms at the table. I shake my head in honest respect. I know I wouldn't have the balls or imagination for this sort of thing. If Sasha is trying to lull me it's working.

Somehow I know Sasha has a card from Coca Cola with his name on it but nothing that Atlanta ever issued. The performance is spectacular right up to the point where he confides, after thumping the table, that a man can take shade in the spread of a Turkish woman's ass. I must admit I lost it then and started to laugh but saved myself with the napkin faking a choking fit.

I rebounded almost immediately and apologized for interrupting. Sasha knows his spell is broken and makes his move on the women, who go with him, leaving tweedy, horse face alone and a little winsome. Pope has been beaten at his own game. Finally, he smiles to himself and joins the group departing for the show, which is now in progress.

I consider Pope and wonder why he would want to be me.

Chapter Six - 10:40 P.m. - MS Albianna off Puerto Rico

The Veil Falls

Death, what is it really? The end, of course, peace, tranquility, escape from the tortures of this life? A route to a better place. I wondered what Jerry thought it was? He sprawled across the small table, that held the Walther, just beyond his grasp. Sightless blue eyes evaluated the wall. Blood pooled about the bottom of the table still bright but growing black. Jerry had hesitated, why? Had he thought it was me returning? How many people would know the location of the new cabin three decks from the old one.

Megel lay on his back. His mouth open asif he were about to sing an aria. Crossed hands covered the hole in his chest, over his heart, where blood welled between lifeless fingers. I wonder if he sees God as his life is blasted from him? His eyes and face seem to reflect amazement.

The electronic units Jerry was using are smashed beyond recognition. My immediate thought is the Chinese. How though? There was no electric link between the camera and this cabin. However, in fairness the camera was ours. It was easy to identify.

I should enter and close their eyes, put something
over their faces. Do the decent thing. This time
unfortunately, I did what the book said. I closed the
door with a soft click and left, having removed my
fingerprints from the surface.

I tried to balance the enormity of the loss. Reading
was a good man and my friend. The bile of rage
roared to my mouth. My first thiught was that the
Chinese were going to pay for this one. Then I
thought perhaps the person who shot the elder spy
wore the snake ring of the Avengers. Then there
was something else, what? Pimple or someone who
was behind the Pimple. Who, Sasha or Legev?. The
cast of characters seemed to increase with ever step.

Clear your mind and think. Anyone who even
looked dangerous to Reading, coming through that
door, would have been killed without a by your
leave. Perhaps the assailant had a key? No, even
then the deadbolt bar would have stopped an
intruder. Who Knew the knock sequence? The
calculations became a little easier as I considered
the potential.

   1) The ring people were accident prone. They
      would have waited unless one of them
      slipped up and Jerry forced the situation. That
      didn't seem likely.

2) Sasha was with me. That put him out of the
   picture.
3) Pimple was in the room and too stupid to work
   out the situation. Even then the whole thing was
   done with three shots. How good would the
   eunuch be with agun? Shirl had said very good.
   Pimple would work on hatred though. I saw his
   face before he tried to kill me. It was a stone
   killer's job. The killing was necessary not
   personal. So not Pimple.
4) The Chinese yes. they had the ability and the
   competence. They could get the information
   about empty cabins and would probably have a
   heat detector to see which one was occupied.
   Then there was that post card worth a million
   and a quarter US. The enemy flew the Chinese
   flag.

Finally , who else were on ship, who wanted the
card? The Pakistanis and many others would be
pleased to get the information. The game went
round and round. What to do?.

First things first. One, to my cabin and the Luger.
At least it would give me some defense.

Two, find out where the Chinese were. The names
should be clear on the list. Remember

,however, they looked white and would probably carry Caucasian names.

Fear caught at me and I started to think about holeing up in my cabin or the one that was now Jerry and Megel's tomb. Hide until tomorrow when Harry Breakleaf and the British Virgin Islands Constabulary would get aboard and I could do a search. At least I knew where Pimple was or had been . Harry and I could work out the rest. I had to stay alive.

Unfortunately that little matter was already being taken care off in a rather convoluted way.

The two men who exited the service locker were huge. They stood over six two or three, weighing in at a minimum of two hundred fifty pounds. Both men were Yakusa. A little of the standard tattooing which identified them showed below the dark suit sleeve of the tallest. My immediate reaction was to run. To hell with it, the best retreat was a good attack.

"Yes! ' I addressed them as if they were working for me. I hoped they couldn't hear my teeth chatter. The mastodons stopped. A third hidden in the vestibule came out to see what the hold up was.

"Our master would like to speak to you." said the largest.

"Do you treat your master's guests in such a shabby manner?" I accused.

"We meant no disrespect." The big one bowed looking for some support from his associate, who bowed also but had no input. I returned the bow but made it to a subservient individual.

"Hai, direct me to your master," I commanded. The three men formed a wedge around me . I immediately increased my pace to make them work. Almost leading them. This caused some consternation . We arrived on the imperial suites deck and stopped before a door. I stood for a moment, then looked over to the heavy faced leader as if to say 'Do you expect me to open the door myself.' There was hesitation.

"It is best if we insure your …."

"You wish to search me, excellent! I would expect nothing less" I lifted my arms and spread my legs. The shake down was quick, efficient and unobtrusive as possible. They found nothing but did remove my fountain pen. It was just a fountain pen but well I guess I couldn't blame them.

The door was now opened. The soft, high pitched sound of Japanese traditional music offered a background. The man who sat cross legged behind a black lacquered table was dressed in a gray silk robe. Above the edge of the silk showed a uniquely beautiful dragon tattooed on his wide chest.

The emerald eyes of the reptile seemed to follow the movements of those in the room.

The leader had a round cold face. The eyes were old perhaps in evil or perhaps just jaded. Black quarts-like pebbles evaluated me from across the room. Thin brows mounted the eyes below a broad flat forehead, which was pockmarked by acne. The cheeks, were clear but jowly. The mouth was fleshy but a prop. It worked on command but seemed to be separate from the man. His chin disappeared into his neck which was very short. Broad powerful shoulders extended outward to sinewy arms and stubby hands. I noticed the little finger on the right hand was missing. Someone had been bad.

I walked over to the table with a powerful nonchalance, which I did not feel and stopped, looking down at the Yakusa.

"You wish to see me?" I asked. The voice was arrogant and it brought his eyes up minutely. I think he liked balls. He smiled lightly but it disappeared as quickly as it had appeared.

"Sit, I don't look up at people." He said in passable English.

I made a big production of sitting at my age it wasn't all fake. If you're not used to it sitting cross legged can be torture. However, I figured as long as we talked, I would probably be alive. It also allowed me to get close enough to jump him in the last desperate moment. That would really be funny. I figured to have the man laugh himself to death watching me attempt the attack. Kind of like watching an elephant getting out of a mud hole, trust me on this.

"You do not die. I find this most disturbing." He started.

"My name Is Michael, D'Iverville McFurson I am a marketing executive. My business here is a photo shoot .' Proper manners must be applied. 'I do not have the honour of knowing your name. Living is something one does. The alternatives are less pleasant." A second smile.

"You may know an associate of mine? His name was Isu Harada." He looked at my face to see the reaction. I figured that would be the tie in so was not surprised.

"I remember a Harada. He bought and sold children. There is little honour in his memory for me." There, you go do something with that.

The eyes came up cold and dead. I thought I was about to join Harada, but no. He purses his lips.

"You may call me Mr. Hai." Mr. Yes, I guess that works. Very few people would say anything else to this animal and live, that is. 'My men throw you over the side of this ship."

"They seem to have gotten the wrong man. As you can see."

"No! You have a number of people who want you dead. The fat screaming individual who cut the ropes on the platform. Also a number of Chinese security people." He said as if it was second nature to have that knowledge.

"Have your people killed any one else this trip or would that be prying?" I smiled. If he killed Jerry, then humor or not, he was going to die. He must have perceived the danger.

"I have a Ruger pistol centered on your back. If you twitch, you will find out just how unpleasant the alternatives are. However, no one else disturbed my serenity on this voyage."

"May I ask, why you would wish to kill a man you do not know, for no reason? If it's revenge for Harada, while there is little honor in it, at least it has some reason." I didn't think he gave a rats ass about Harada alive or dead.

Mr. Hai , looked uncomfortable.

"In seven years I have taken no vacation. I come here and find you. You can understand my discomfort." He said , The frustration of being hidden down here would drive me nuts. Mr. Hai must have suffered being trapped down here unable to take pictures or look at the sights.

 "Unless you are selling children I have no interest in you at all." I said honestly. This caught him and I knew it. He knew I wasn't lying. Hai san couldn't take the chance. His hard eyes evaluated his hands.

 "Also as you can understand my organization is aware of the matters as they stand. I carry a monitor. It identifies heat profiles. This allows easy definition of where I am and where I go. In an hour we will be in British waters. My death would become a very unpleasant matter for you.' He didn't like this but he was listening. Hai san fingered my pen I knew I had him. 'On the other hand there are two people who matter very much to me. The result of your death or removal would be unproductive . Your successor might not honor your word.' He looked at me with new interest. This gave him power and he liked being in charge. 'I suggest we make bargain. I will see you have no more problems on this vacation. You will forget about me and allow me to take care of my business with the Chinese. This may also remove your other concerns.. I believe this is a reasonable way of clearing up the difficulty". I smiled and he smiled back .

He looked up now and our eyes met. Hai decided that I could be trusted. I thought I needed a little more, so I went for it.

"There is also the matter of responsibility for the actions of your men. Blame must fall properly in order to secure Wai." I thought I had gone too far but this allowed him to accept responsibility and make amends without losing face.

"It seems I owe you a life." He said.

"Yes!"

"The terms are agreeable. Will you have sake" he asked. To refuse would be an insult.

"Of course. "

He moved a hand. One of the men who had been waiting placed a small tray between us. On it was a tapered bottle of sake and two glasses. Mr. Hai poured himself.

"The Emperor!" I offered the toast. He nodded his agreement.

"Your queen" he made the gesture and I drank the rice wine which tasted slightly like beer.

"We have little in common McFurson San."

"This is true Hai San. Perhaps because we are two ends of the same pond there must be the harmony of our competition.

" Yes. You are Canadian but you speak with the heart of a Japanese. We see all British as the same. Your people see each part of the whole, as a whole onto its self. This is strange for us. All Japanese are Japanese. All white men are white men.

"Perhaps we are unique." I suggested indicating the two of us. He smiled then.

"Yes, McFurson San perhaps, but remember we are from different parts of the pond."

"Do you know where these Chinese are on the ship?"

"No!" he lied but that wasn't his problem it was mine.

" Then Hai San I must look for them." I rose to leave without being bidden.

" I will send Kuno with you to insure your safety." He offered. Kuno was the leader of my honor guard. Kuno had a small forehead and dull brown eyes set in a featureless mask .

" The matter is international. There might be repercussions that would damage your wai. Better

perhaps that you not be associated with this
situation and enjoy your holiday."
"Agreed but remember I have many friends." He
reminded me of my personal survival.
" I will not forget." I rose and bowed. He did the
same. I offered my hand. He took it hesitantly but
with a iron grasp which left my hand smarting.
"Good luck! Is that the proper statement?" He
asked hesitantly
"Yes! Good day." I turned and left.
I knew Kuno was just behind me. This was
expected but it was going to be a problem.

One, I knew in my heart, Mr. Hai whatever his
name was, would not want me around. There was
too much potential for damage. The British
Government might want to talk to him. At the
moment I held him hostage. Kuno would try to
kill me. Try, OK. Rationalization is always the
better part of stupidity.
First, back to my cabin and the Luger. Once it
was in my hands I would feel substantially better.
As I walked around I thought about the pure
percentages of me being on a ship with the head
of the Japanese mob. It was mind boggling. Or

was he involved with the search for the post card and of course, the bag of money. After all a million was a million and he could be attached to the Japanese Government but I didn't think so.

I of course could go to the Italian Captain. That would blow my cover and open Pandora's box. If he was smart he would place me in chains and blame me for good old Reading's murder. In this way he might bypass the international incident.

One of the cabin stewards came up to me on my deck. I had seen him before and knew he was responsible for Cherie-Lee's cabin.

He might be from Indonesia, I thought. The crews on these ships were made up of 104 nations and spoke more languages then the UN. He offered a note.

'Please come and see me.' It said it was signed by Cherie-Lee . Cherie must be desperate she never wrote anything. However , it was her tiny scrawl .

"You come?" The little man asked with an uncertain look.

"Yes I come!" he nodded and smiled, but my mind was screaming Blind side Blind side , Blind Side.

The steward lead me to the door and knocked lightly three times, then once more and said a word which sounded like mandarin for tea. What the hell?

The door opened and I felt the gun barrel in my back. I had found the Chinese or their representatives. If the Americans were using fake CIA types, maybe Chinese State Security was also using in-betweens.

I am shoved into the room. The door closes. I set to spring but stop as a soft old English voice cuts in.

"Ah, Mr. McFurson you've finally arrived like a good little chap." The woman in the wheel chair had to be seventy but the sharp little hawks eyes watched me like a cat might a mouse. Her tone her movements, her look were all Caucasian and very English. Something was different, I could not pick it up but it was there. She looked like your standard British grandma, white hair, a thin pinched face, a thin nose and a little squarish mouth.

"I'm pleased, you're pleased. Is this a kidnapping?" I asked as if I were very nervous.

Our company will pay for the models." I presume
they have Cherie. My mind is screaming stupid,
stupid, stupid.

"Mr. McFurson we were hoping we could get
this matter settled. Now with dear old Jerry's
death, I suspect you realize a report will have to
be made. I'm afraid you've been very naughty
and that will have to come out." The tea biscuit
parlance was like someone scolding a small boy. I
could care less. This crap might work on a public
school git. However, when my sainted grandma
Sykes screamed at Harold and I for stealing
cookies, we just stood hang head until she lost
steam, promised to be good and stole more
cookies.

Dear Jerry, did she know him? Perhaps in the
world, as we call our small piece of hell where
spys lived and died, she might. She was
intimating there was more than that between them
as if she was on his team. I wait for it.
" Now you must listen closely". She was talking
to a small boy. I wasn't him.

"Its a beautiful day for skeet." She said very
exactly. I am to infer from this she is a

member of the firm, as it is the first line of the
day code. If this little deal was British Jerry
would have known. Maybe if it were a European
thing or Asian but we had very little out there
now.

For a moment I hesitate. Then I see Visitor One
from the exchange, hidden in the bathroom which
is in the far end of the cabin to the right. No I
think not.

"Do you shoot skeet.?" I asked stupidly.

"I find none of this humorous Mr. McFurson.
You are being a very stubborn boy and we have
very little time. You realize they will find Jerry
soon and then we must move quickly. We've
already been in touch with Breakleaf in Road
Town.

"Now! Its a beautiful day for skeet."

"You're Chinese. I didn't see it at first but you
are oriental." I point out

"Ah well it might have been easier. We are
looking for a post card, brightly coloured, with a
yellow fish on one side."

My mental mind control inset was coming into
place . A range of items were disappearing from
my memory while my mind and body became

totally concentrated on escape. The change must
have shown.

"We could of course do very unpleasant things
to you Mr. McFurson. However there is the noise
and of course your programming has more or less
made you useless, at this moment." Whoever she
was she was a player and knew the rules of
engagement.

If I had accepted her as the real thing then of
course I would have opened up. Having closed
my mind to them there was no information and I
had no value. Goody, I was redundant, at a point
where it might be the last thing I would
remember.

" If I had the time of course it might be very
interesting. You can get a great deal from them,
even the small ones like this, if you work hard." I
am talked about as if I do not exist. The
statements are made to the room in general, as a
teacher might. However, you will not make
noise." Grandma said with assurance.

"No?" I ask just to challenge

"No." The old blue veined hand waves just
slightly. The curtain like door on the bathroom is
opened wide. Cherie's white naked body is
sprawled on the floor. The delicate Chinese girl

who had waited on each and every one of the
senators words, now holds an expensive Colt
automatic with silencer on the sprawled model.

"If she's dead so what?" I said off the point of
my mind which was balancing into attack mode.

"Show him." Madam butterfly kicked Cherie
viciously with her small foot. Cheri groaned and
then whimpered in complaint. She was obviously
drugged. I wondered how they got her to write the
letter I would figure a gun would work just fine.

"Kill her!" I said like a surgeon cutting a limb.

"No we're all professionals but I know your
little friend has value to you and you will do what
you can to keep her alive." She tells the truth.

"Please take off your clothing Mr. McFurson.
And please nothing quick. We can remove them
after you're dead too. She began to knit.

I removed the cotton shirt and passed it over.
The two Chinese and the steward look into every
crevice of the clothing. I continue to remove
clothing until I am in my underwear. I hesitate
only from some last flake of modesty.

"Those too, I'm afraid." Says Grandma. The
black shorts are passed over and given very
special evaluation.

The next phase starts with nose ,eyes and throat.
My ears are checked minutely. I have had
physicals which were less well conducted. I was
checked between my fingers and between my
toes. I look at the Chinese girl who frowns
slightly as if she has seen better. I am not
beautiful anymore pity. Having looked under my
nails and other likely locations, some of which
were very ingenious, they stood off for a moment.
If I actually had been carrying anything they
certainly would have found it. Of course when
the information is on dots or small computer
chips this sort of thing is absolutely necessary.
"Nothing Madame. "Visitor One says. He had a
squarish but small face, with cold black eyes, thin
features and very bad breath. He will be the
leader or at least second in command.

"I do not suspect I could offer you money could
I?" The woman said.

"How much?" I kept the conversation going
because I had a feeling what was coming next and
I was not looking forward to it.

"Don't toy with me Mr. McFurson. I am in no
mood for your attempts at humour."
I simply looked at her as neutrally as possible,
naked in the middle of the room.

"Very well.' 250,000 "

"Pounds?" I asked.

"Dollars."

"This must be some fish.' I say as if considering the offer. 'He might have mailed it?" I offered. I knew that if I lead them to the prize I was dead. They would never let me out of here to get it.

Why do people always hit me in the kidneys? It was very light but very painful. Visitor One went right off my Christmas list.

"Seeing you want to play, we will play, bend over Mr. McFurson." Grandma sounded excited.

I remember the face of Dan Marino in the last game of the 1999 season. It was a playoff game and it was a disaster. Everything had gone wrong. Dan had thrown two pics ,I could remember. Had the ball torn away from him for a fumble. No one was catching the ball, even the punter missed a kick and that became a touchdown as well. In the end the Dolphins were getting shellacked 62 to 7 and they were doomed. Dan's look embraced all of it. The anger, disgrace, self loathing that I felt now. The next few minutes will remain in my mind as the worst I have ever spent. When it was over and the findings which were nil were reported, the elderly leader became very agitated

. We were close to British waters she couldn't stop the ship unless she sank it and I did not believe she would do that.

"May I dress?' I asked, not expecting to be allowed to.

"Oh my yes, please do." She said thinking as she spoke.

I put my clothing on and waited with a second Colt thirty eight pointed at my stomach.

"Go to Mr. McFurson's cabin and search it again Martin," So Visitor One had a name. 'Take Elan with you." The steward moved toward the door. 'You may also take Mr. McFurson . Remember young man we have this lady here who will die instantly should you do anything stupid."

This was an interesting change of events. Had I been her, I never would have let me out of the room. Why do it? Well, it was a gamble I figured. If grandma went back to China without her prize, the results would be too horrible to consider. The Chinese weren't big on failure. So I was to escape and perhaps lead them to the goal. That would make sense. It would be easy to place bugs on all my clothing. This whole episode could just be a sham. I leave the room, surprise, someone falls or whatever and that's that. They sit in the cabin and watch. I go to ground with the prize, then they take it back.

The only other explanation is that while they search my room, I will become agitated or look at the location of the post card, thereby giving it away. Stupidity is out of the question.

Elan opens the door and we leave.

The corridor is empty, this is checked. I am bracketed, the gun is in my back. The bullet might pass through me but light weapons have one reason for being. Once the projectile enters the body cavity they bounce off the ribs under usual circumstances and roll tearing up everything else. I will be good we will see.

We reach my cabin. Martin has the credit card key which he slips into the slot and obtains a green light. I am moved into the door way. Martin turns on the lights without effect. He moves forward to find the lamp . The movement in the room is imperceptible but very real. Martin is locked in mortal combat with someone. In the moment Elan looks away, I turn and using my weight, I jam him against the frame. The steward has made the mistake of being between the door frame and my body. I jam my fingers directly into his eye sockets, a la the Three Stooges. However, while this is done for comic effect with the fingers retracted, I drive in full length to the brain. My other hand short chops his throat while my left knee collides with his privates . Rule one, if you're going to do hand to hand win. Rule two, always have a second act. The gun which was lowered drops nervelessly from his hand. Elan, now mortally wounded, brings his hand up to protect himself. I grab his hair and jerk the head forward while bringing my fist down on the base of his neck twice with all the force in my body. I hear the snap and let the corpse fall, while I scoop up the thirty eight and turn to face the room. I snap on the bathroom light, which is to my left and watch the last moments of Martin's life slip away. Kuno has him at arm's length, above his head strangling him slowly. Martin smashes away at his larger and more lethal opponent. The beating Kuno takes would have killed me. Finally, he shakes the enemy agent like a dead rat and drops him.

His lifeless eyes, surrounded by his featureless face turns to me. He is breathing like a wolf after a kill, in great gulps. However, this becomes more controlled. He had been here for me of course. I shiver at the thought but I would not have entered , maybe?

I do not point the gun at him but I ask politely if he will turn on the lamp. He does reluctantly. In the light he is a much better target. I move into the room dragging Elan with me and close the door.

Kuno backs up but only slightly, changing his footing. Question, can he reach me before I kill him? Question can I kill him before he reaches me?

I bow slightly which is returned.

" Tell your master his debt is paid. He owes me nothing but I am grateful to him." The flat hard face does not change but he nods.

"Now leave." We circle as he heads for the door. I back into the room stepping over Martin. He opens the door and leaves without further ado.

Chapter Seven - 8:25 A.m. Her Majesty's Secret
Service, North American Section, London England.

To See And Be Seen

Rain drizzles down on the old cobblestones that
surround the oak in the middle of Granny's court.
Theodore (Granny) Boothby-Staters looked out at
the ancient tree and counted the remaining leaves.
There were five today, tomorrow the count would
drop again. The tree would be rid of useless mouths
and ready for winter.

Granny was missing people who could not be
replaced. They could, of course, if he took someone
from elsewhere. The Northern Ireland situation was
cooling down. Given there was no massive reversal
in the peace process. There would be so many good
people available. Perhaps, one of them could take
over from Jerry.

Damn McFurson! How could anyone who seemed
to do all the right things and have such phenomenal
luck, be such a trip wire for his staff?

Jerry Reading, there was another letter he would
have to write. The body brought back for burial.
Reading's son had cried on the phone, at least there
would be someone to see Jerald off. After Granny
had partaken of the usual abysmal funeral. A quick
stop in to hand over the posthumous DSO without a

name on it. Something the boy could hold on to. Would he want to? Would it matter?

Jerry was a good man, a little eccentric, but good. At the moment his death was simply the worst thing that could happen.

Why in God's name would he go after the CIA and the Chinese External Security People. The transfer would occur somewhere else, surely. Perhaps not, Langley did not seem to know about this whole thing or at least that was the feed back he was getting on the subject. You never knew what the Yanks were doing or would do anymore.

Granny moved around his desk and opened Jerry Reading's file . In the next second, he took a Players Extra Mild from his gold cigarette case and lit it with his gold Zippo. Sitting, he dragged the smoke deep into his lungs and then exhaled slowly, joyously.

Couldn't smoke at home with the new baby, but that was a small loss. His Oxford Don features softened. An elegant but strong hand touched the line of his perfectly combed golden hair.

Deedre, his new princess, had his eyes and nose, poor thing. The prattle that came out of her was continuous. Granny would feed her late at night to let Sil sleep. Once she had her bottle and before she slept, her highness would talk to him and he to her.

Jerry's picture brought Granny back to his office and the rain outside. Reading was showing off for McFurson. He knew it. Not that there was anything sexual to it, just proving he was senior man. Stupid! In fairness how do you top being thrown off a ship and then beating it into port?

The CIA, FBI, US Coast Guard, the American Foreign office and others too numerous to mention, were presently giving Granny through Sir Mortimer Bray the head of the Secret Service endless pain over the whole thing.

Why was McFurson in Puerto Rico? What was the problem? What open file was it in aid of? You're not landing another bunch of SAS are you? No, we're going to let master agent do the job. Fat bloody chance that.

McFurson's death at this point would be a welcome development. No! Can't say that. McFurson of course was top priority. More because they couldn't figure out who was behind whatever was going on . This Toad person was part of it. Michael was correct in thinking the man was only a pawn.

The Avengers of the Ring were a completely different thing. The problem Jerry had come up with after McFurson had dealt with Au Clair on St. Martin was far more specific. A situation that Granny had following up on with the help of the Dutch and others. Success though important, was difficult to obtain. There were leaks that had to be stopped

If there were some ultra-secret organization who had been running Europe since the Crusades, Granny was surprised they didn't bump off Hitler. Maybe they were in with him. Given the computerized competence of the ever increasing number of international spy agencies, someone would have to know about this lot.

Yet even Granny felt the chill created by this information. He had seen too much, knew too much. How many people had been killed? Were airplanes going down because of these mad men? He knew people disappeared, had untoward accidents. The CIA had almost trademarked the heart attack.

Granny had had a really good laugh when they got all the past heads of the CIA and KGB together and everyone denied everything. Of course, there were no kidnappings, no muted deaths and more specifically no cold war. What a great steaming lorry load of shit.

Bugger McFurson! At the moment he was trapped in a room with two dead bodies. The Canadian was about to take a risk that under normal circumstances would be out of the question. Unfortunately Granny could do nothing about the situation on the ship. There was no one to intervene. At the worse he was looking at another huge international incident. If he survived, McFurson was done, he could retire or Granny would fire him, this was far too much. .

First, Granny had to make sure what Reading was doing. He could read lips. Had Jerry picked up something in the conversation between the Senator and his associate or the girl? Something that made the post card with its yellow fish important to British interests. How important he wondered? Reading might have something of real value and it was up to McFurson to get it through. The Canadian of course would do what he bloody well pleased and perhaps would lose the chance of a lifetime.

One thing was abysmally certain the Chinese didn't kill Jerry Reading . Granny knew who and it wasn't a bunch of European assassins either.

The only thing that took the edge off his discomfort with this whole matter; was the knowledge that the Americans were in equal difficulties. The listening devise the Russians placed in the wall of the conference room, National Defense building in Washington, had made the national press. Wasn't that a beautiful bit of work and the Americans were red faced.

Then, of course, there was the silly cow from CISIS in Canada; who was leaving top level classified information for her lover, indiscreetly in her unlocked auto.

To top it off, the Poles were throwing ten Russians out for spying. He had to laugh. Granny could imagine the venomous exchange following that bit of post cold war idiocy

He couldn't laugh a great deal though. There were the daily press releases about the myriad of moles in his own firm. University professors who worked for the East Germans ,secretaries with keys to the vault and so on. Most of them had been turned years before. A few of those unveiled startled even him.

Granny smiled softly. He remembered a story he had heard of an Italian General. After an absolutely

horrible and disastrous military exercise. The Italian
said his one consolation was that there were other
armies and of course other generals with problems
of the same kind and magnitude. It was originally
told as a joke, as the Ities tended to bumble. Granny
believed the Gererali was correct though. The other
side was never perfect.

Now he must think. Margaret would take over
Puerto Rico. Breakleaf will meet the Albianna and
hopefully pick up the pieces because he felt that
McFurson's luck might have run out this time.

At least in Reading's case there would be a
balancing of the tables. He picked up the phone on
his desk. It was answered in the hive below him.
"Tell T section I will need someone . In about a
fortnight, I would think. Perhaps before. Thank
you."

Now all he had to do was get Sir Mortimer to sign
a death warrant for another human being, there by,
removing the responsibility from Granny and
making the world safer for humanity. Not bloody
likely.

11:20 Room 49, Athens deck MS Albianna

I had stripped naked and placed my old clothing on the chair. This removed me from any contact bugs in the clothing. I then searched my own cavities to find a couple of new attachments. These joined the clothing on the chair . I should be cut off now from their homing devices. I then moved Martin and Elan about the room. In Cherie's cabin they would be looking at pinpoints of light on a screen. Mine would be found in the chair. There was no camera in my room. I scanned the place immediately after Kuno left. Hopefully they would believe that the search was still in progress.

I figured twenty minutes would be about right before the next act. Dressed in a white open face shirt and my blue tropical weight Brooks Brothers suit. I placed the Luger with its silencer attached, inside the waist band of my pants.

The Bushmills from the small mickey, I had secreted with the gun, tasted wonderful. The gray metal elephant contained the components of the Luger. I knew no one had found the weapon or played with it, therefor the whisky should be alright. The gentle burning of the raw alcohol helped. Then a quick report to Granny over the internet on the lap top. I moved my lifeless companions again to give the semblance of a search for the watchers.

At exactly 11:20, I exited my room. Kuno was not lurking nearby, that was a start. I made my way down the empty neutral smelling corridor. Placing myself just back form the door of Cherie-Lee's room I removed the Luger but kept it hidden under my jacket.

At this time there were very few people in the corridors. The majority were up at the midnight buffet grazing, as the crew like to define the pig out each night. I ask myself, 'what am I doing here?', but have no good answer.

The heat sensor I had appropriated from Elan, told me approximately where everyone was in the cabin.

I knocked three times, then once more and said the word for tea in mandarin. There was a soft return from the other side of the door. The door opened inward. I placed the muzzle of the silenced Luger against the barrier about heart level, compress the handle safety and pull the trigger. The nine millimeter slug was undeterred by the light wood door. There was a grunt and I felt the weight fall away from the other side. As the door opened, the bathroom came into view. The little Chinese girl lifted her silenced thirty-eight to return fire. I had already completed the police officers two step and was in shooting stance. The Luger hummed three times. Her body jumped like a puppet and bounced off the wall to crumple onto the bathroom floor.

Rounding the door I found Visitor Two dead in a heep. Grandma was trying to get her gun from under the blanket covering her legs. I swung with all my might and hit her on the jaw. I made sure she was out cold and disarmed. Then I stopped for a moment.

The door closed with the weight of Visitor Two against it. I stood there heaving. I had been lucky but it had been well thought out and I had the components correct. However, had any of them been out of place I would have died

I checked Grandma to see if she was still breathing and was gratified to realize she was. A tuff old bird this one.

I tied Grandma to the bed. Then gagged her with a piece of wood from the bathroom. I knew without looking she would have at least one and probably two cyanide pills in her teeth. I had to hope she would be unable to remove them with the gag or bite down on them with the wood inserted.

Finally, I went to the bathroom and looked down at Cherie's full body sprawled on the floor. I hesitantly put my finger on her neck. There was a pulse but it was sluggish. She drooled a little and made a soft mewing sound.

It was at this point that the enormity of the past hour's events hit me. I sat down on the toilet and looked at the scene. If we have karma, mine seemed to leave my body and see the situation from a different angle, complete neutrality for a moment . Then I placed my face in my hands and breathed deeply for a few moments.

I had killed without reason. I had attacked a group of people who would have harmed me but had I hidden until the authorities had come aboard at Road town I could have by passed the slaugther. The book says run. The book says take advantage of any weakness. The book does not say frontal attack.

There were no heroics though. I just knew that if I ran Cherie-Lee would have paid big time. I loved Cherie-Lee, she was my friend and I had gotten her into this. In a circumstance such as this you do and worry about the results afterward. The gentleman's code I was taught from youth, stayed with me. I could not run.

I had killed a woman, twenty something, a child, beautiful and intelligent, God! The butterfly hands would never flutter again. I looked into her blank frightened dead face. I see the evil I am and hate myself.

To top it off, I smacked a woman who could have

been my mother in the mush. Talk about your hero type.

Of course what I had done was the only thing possible. All of these people would have killed me in a second for a post card.

What to do? Well Cherie first.

I lifted Cherie-Lee's dead weight and washed Madame Butterfly's blood from her legs, behind and back. I then put panties on her. This is not an easy thing to do, when there is no motor response and the girl weighs in at 110lbs. I chose a loose summer dress that slides on and place my shoulder under hers to carry her down the corridor.

We exit and run right in to a man and woman who are returning from the deck above. There are stares and a soft command from the woman to leave it alone.

I mumble something about to much too drink and haul Cherie down the corridor to Nome's door. Praying while I knock, Cherie drools on my shoulder. There is a lot of noise and movement then a quick.

" Who the hell is it?" demands the annoyed Nome.
" Its Mike, Cherie is in a bad way, I need some help." The door opens immediately. Nome is dressed in a towel. His naked body glistens with soft golden body hair.

"Christ, what happened?" He takes the other shoulder and helps me carry the drugged model to the still warm bed. Misty looks out of the bathroom naked and open mouthed.

" Someone slipped her a mickey. Some Chinese guy. He had her when I caught up with them in the hall.

"What happened? " He demands again closing the door.

"I suggested he give me the lady or I'd tear his head off."

"Seems to have worked." he quipped.

"Yeah! But she is full of something. Look I don't think she's too bad. Cherie was desperately trying to come around, shaking her head lazily to gain some semblance of reality.

"Why don't we go up find this guy and pound the shit out of him?" No one ever questioned Nome's personal bravery.

"Great , say we go up there and don't find the right Chinese. Can you say law suit? Anyway Cherie needs help and I don't want a lot of bad publicity. Also I don't want anyone in her room. I think they were in there and I want to make sure there are finger prints. If so I don't want them disturbed. We need them. If not I'll clean up and take care of it right." Nome nodded he understood bad publicity and this would mess up the shoot and of course payment for the work. Misty was dressed in shorts and a top . She helped by putting a wet washcloth on Cherie's forehead. How much good it did I don't know. However, it kept her busy and it couldn't hurt.

"Listen,' she says as if having an epiphany. 'I got some stuff maybe it could bring her around?"

"No! you don't give her anything." I snarled.

"She's just trying to help." said Nome softly. Misty looked frightened and hurt.

"Nome we don't know what she has in her, for crying out loud, this isn't the time for chemistry class." Nome nodded

"I know ,don't worry. Now apologize to Misty, then she won't be all hurt. I have to shoot her tomorrow."

"Mist, listen, I am sorry." I put on my charm but after killing three people, there wasn't much left. It's just I'm kind of upset about Cherie. It's been a real tuff little while, also I'm scared we're going to get bad press. I know you mean well but don't please give Cherie anything. It might not go down well with what's inside and make her worse you understand." I thought she just might. She smiled softly and nodded.

"Good." I said " I am going to get the doctor. Then I'll take care of the rest of it. Keep an eye on her."

" No problem." Nome replied

What I was about to do was against every rule in the book and I knew it. I checked the passenger list and made for the deck above mine. The Corinth Deck was the same as the one below. The cabins were the same size. The view was better by a deck but the owner was a past citizen of that fabled Greek city so Corinth was top passenger deck. Except the suites, of course, which were behind the bridge and for the very rich. I kept the Luger out under a towel. If Kuno came at me I was going to punch his ticket. I was at the end of the line. It was a bad time to be near me and I knew it. I could smell blood and would kill with little provocation. It would take me a long time to calm down.

I checked the cabin but the good doctor was not there. This meant a search the ship for him. Then as I turned, Pope dropped down the stairs from the buffet. He had the same hang dog expression, he had had earlier. I wondered what kind of luck he was having with the spy line. I had read an article or heard on radio where single men over a certain age only had sex if they had lots of money or better a certain amount of personal prestige. This was gained either through money, position or its benefits. You'd think being a doctor would give good old Pope a lead. On the other hand he wasn't much to look at. Rusty, thinning red hair waved across the bald spots. His face was long, leathery, like an upside down horse collar. In the center of this sole shaped visage, sprouted a strong north midlands nose, that divided two watery blue eyes, with thin whitening brows. The mouth was large, wet looking and frowning almost to clown proportion. Below that, however, was a strong, rock hard chin. You got the feeling you could trust the man. Then again he also let on he was a spy and that was a patent lie. In reality though we all lied a little to get laid.

"Dr. Pope! I thought I had seen you up here." I started beaming my best, good friend well met smile.

"Oh!" He didn't recognize me. Then it hit him, Doctors are always looking for little details because for the most part their patients lied to them. I guess I jogged a nerve.

His face changed again. He probably figured I had some malady to bring to his attention. It was clear free medical advice was not an option. So I went for his week point, women.

"Listen, I wouldn't bother you but those two sisters were talking to me. They wondered if I knew where you were on the boat. They also gave me their phone number. If you got a pen, Ill give it to you.' I continued smiling as if I was impressed. 'I guess they liked what they saw." I winked and laughed. "Really !" Pope looked surprised and then pensive then well, he smiled too because we all like to be complimented.

"Oh bother, I don't have a piece of paper or a pen.' he patted his pockets franticly. Then he realized we were in front of his cabin. 'Wait we'll go inside and I'll just write that down." The door opened and I was inside.

I sat in a chair while he found a pen and turned, then pulled up short. My face was very far from a smile. The evening was getting to me and my nerves were on end. I had taken one of my high blood pressure pills and it was kicking in but I was still on edge.

"What is this about?" he seemed to brace himself as if I might be interested in robbing him. In a sense I would do that but it was his innocence he would loose not his money."

"You intimated you were a member of the British Secret Service tonight." I said and there was ice in it.

"Oh no. That's just a line for the birds. I mean women like that sort of thing. A little danger and so fourth." He said rubbing his hands together, a little nervous twitch at being caught out.

"Yeah, women are always throwing themselves at me." I was very tired and a little sarcastic.

"You try that sort of line too do you?" He smiled nervously beginning to worry what the hell he was facing.

"Yes! but unfortunately I'm the real thing." I looked up at him.

"Excuse me!" He said as if he hadn't heard me.

"Take a good look kid, I'm Her Majesty's Secret Service. " I said straight up.

"I see, how long have you been involved?" He said in a condescending way. Pope obviously thought I was some poor nut. I didn't fault him.

"No doctor I'm not delusional. I need your help. You're on the call list with the army right? You just went active service again." He looked at me with suspicion and more then a little fear.

"What do you mean? I'm a doctor not one of the lost boys. Get out of here."

"All right doc we'll do it the hard way." He had moved to the door but stopped then and turned thinking perhaps he would see a gun. He might have but I had something far more lethal, the truth.
I read from the faxed sheets I had removed from my pocket.

" Dr. Julius Pope, Captain Sunderland Fusiliers medical'. I read his tag number and continued.

'Father, Peter Pope, contractor, member of the
Masons. Although with a name like yours you
would think it would be the Knights of Columbus.
Your dog's name was Tipper, got hit by a car in
1964. Too bad! Mother, Jane Seymore, seamstress.
Your cousin Albert's queer."

"Good God! Where did you get all that?" he
choked out

"I called up and my people did a check on you.
This is the report. Want to know what you made last
year? I rhymed off the amount.' This really shook
him. Pope sat on the bed and looked at me as if I
was about to kill him.

"Here is a note from your Regimental Commander.
He says you're not a bad medico but a bit of a
bounder. The Regimental Sergeant Major's wife I
believe."

" Fine, I believe you. Good God! You're not even
British. You're American."

"Canadian" I said cold bloodedly. The world is
going to hell isn't it? I haven't got much time will
you help me?"

"You mean I have a choice? "

"Of course. We don't kill people if they don't want
to be a part of things , that is the other guys. Well,
doc what's it to be?" He only hesitated for a
moment. I will give him that.

 "Yes, I suspect so. If I don't have to kill anyone or take a parcel ashore. What is it all about? Will I have a gun? Am I in danger?" Now for something really laughable. I wouldn't have this guy behind me with a gun, if my life depended on it. He might be a good doctor and all but he might decide to live his fantasies and I couldn't chance that.

" No gun! Everything I tell you, everything you see, the people you meet, don't exist and never have. I don't exist. It's all national secrets right from the get go. Agreed?"

"Yes, I see,.alright."

" Good. First you're going to see a woman. She was given some drugs to keep her quiet. I got these bottles from the people who used them. "

" These are in Chinese ."

" I thought the smell might give some idea."

" Well no. If I see her I can tell you more."

'The people you're going to meet with the woman have nothing to do with the service, so your the doctor that's it. The second patient is a woman of seventy. She has a lot of information we want. You have to keep her alive for an hour or so until my people from Road Town come on board and take her off. That's it. After that you're clear. You go back to your vacation and you forget everything. Period."

"What am I to call you?" He asked as if he thought
the answer might be Mr. X or something.

"Mike McFurson" I offered my hand. He smiled
and took it

"Julius Pope." He said.

Cherie-Lee, it seemed, was a little worse for wear
but she would come around fine. "

"We went back to her cabin and I stopped Julius
with a hand gesture. The Luger came out. I could
see his face change. It was simultaneous to that he
saw the hole in the door.

" Look there seems to be a bullet hole in the door."
he cautioned.

" I know, I put it there." I said.

" I see." He looked a little green.

Opening the door we went in gun first. The old
woman was awake. Her cold little eyes watched me.

" This is the patient?' he asked astounded, 'You
must untie her, if she is to survive."

" She stays tied . She tried to kill me, amongst other
things, earlier this evening. Watch yourself around
her hands. She might have something hidden. I
didn't have much time for a search. "

He placed his stethoscope on Grandma's frail
chest.

"She seems alright but breathing might be a
problem." Julius was thorough.

"Listen she had at least one cyanide pill in her back teeth. I want her alive." He seemed a little more placated until he looked into the bathroom.

"Good God!" He said going white.

"Don't worry about them,' I indicated the two bodies heaped in the bathroom, 'they aren't going anywhere." Pope looked at the carpet then and at me. I can say, I didn't like the look.

"If it helps, they had the redhead, she means something to me. They also killed my senior agent and his assistant. In this case it was me or them. Normally, I would have run but sometimes you can't."

Chapter Eight- 9:10 Am, Breakleaf's Cottage ,In the hills of Tortola, British Virgin Islands, British West Indies.

Grabbing The Moment

Before me the Atlantic spread royal blue all the way to Africa. Small Cays baked in the 80 degree heat. To my left was the box like beige cottage, which was Breakleafs's fortress of the old Raj. This in one of its last remaining territories. Territories mind, 'Yes we have no colonies we have no colonies today.' The British Government had felt, with so few holdings left under British rule, the term territories was more appropriate.

I sit resplendent in a semicircle of trees. These cup the off shore breeze, as it races up the face of the island to the top, like an over exuberant mountain climber. The wind off the water explodes through the leaves cooling the occupant of this bower. At the same time it surrounds him with the speech of trees which is closely aligned with elfin words, the laughter of far off chimes of a midsummer night's eve.

I sat in my orange Speedo boxer and a cheap

T-shirt, my body in a state of recline. A tall glass of ginger ale tinkled with the impacts of half a dozen ice cubes in my fingers. A soft rendition of Bahama Mama wafted to me over the wind.

I was relaxed as I have never been. It was a good time for reflection while Breakleaf did the donkey work.

Grandma was in hospital under guard. A small military jet would be out to pick her up. I wondered if she was worth it all but head office must think so. I would be interested in finding out just who she is and what her tie in with the Chinese might be?

It had taken six of Superintendent Winston's constables to get Toad out of his little hole of a cabin. Almost all of them carried some kind of wound. In the end, they used pepper spray. I also get the idea one of the constables had a belly full and clubbed the fat eunuch into submission. Winston followed Nelson's eye on that matter.

The six bodies were a real problem. The ship is told they are ill. The ship's owners have a coronary by way of the captain, the ship's doctor and so forth. Breakleaf, on the behalf of the Governor, takes full responsibility. The Italians are somewhat placated, as no one seems to be asking about the people, and they have no next of kin registered but want a complete follow-up. Harry smiles winningly and says the follow-up will be complete. How he will provide this miracle, I am not told. The cabins in question are put off limits as part of the crime scene, for the day. While a group of our people, sent in from head office, clean up the blood and other nasty reminders of my passing through. The bodies come off as if they are all ill and are placed in ambulances, which look somewhat like hearses. Breakleaf saves me from this quagmire and whisks me away from it to this oasis while he smoothes it over with the Governor, who also knows who the hell I am and isn't amused.

Pope and I spend a quiet, if tense, hour and a half until the pilot boat can come aside and the local constabulary arrive. He is, for the most part, quiet, as if pondering life or is just plain scared. I was, why shouldn't he be?

He asks about life in the world of espionage and so on, more to make conversation than to obtain information. I don't say much. In the end, Breakleaf knocks the agreed number of knocks, I say:

"It's a lovely day for skeet."

"If the wind holds", quotes Harry.

"And the light." I finish the phrase of the day and

they are let in led by Burtie Kelman, the local M.O.
Pope and he shake hands like Stanley and
Livingstone, then go into a doctoral huddle over the
patient. Harry wants to know who, or what, Pope is.
I give him the quick basics. Burtie takes over. I
watch the changing of the guard with interest.
Having nothing left to do, Pope receives one of
Harry's bloody 'well done' and a patented hand
shake. The doctor comes out in the hall looking like
he has moved up to the field marshal. He comes
over, a little unsure, and offers his hand, which I
take.

"Suspect, I should thank you for giving me a chance
to have my fantasy. No matter how abjectly
horrible it was." He says with a little smile.
"Don't thank me. You just did your bit.
Remember, it didn't happen." I say a little too
abruptly.

"Well, until next time, then. Oh! I suspect there
won't be a next time, will there?" He nods and
moves off a little sadly. However, I know better. I
may have opened a whole new career for good, old
Dr. J. Pope. I knew Granny's insatiable need for
new people and the fact that a single doctor would
fit right into that framework. An unattached man,
able

to be part of international conferences. No, I thought. Good old Pope might rue the day he told a lie about being a spy and then let me con him into becoming one. As my grandfather used to say, 'Watch out, you may get what you wish for'. I consider that the punishment suits the crime.

Finally, Harry's khaki-clad, six foot-two, footballer's form, extricates itself from his Volkswagen Golf and comes over to take the chair next to me.

"I guess a day's work well done." I said a little bit tentatively.

Breakleaf laughs a deep 'woof', takes the proffered drink from his live in servant, who appears as if by magic and downs half of it.

"What a bloody, horrible mess he says,' shaking his full head of brown hair. His intelligent, unshakable eyes come to rest on me. I watched the smile start under his bushy moustache.

"So, how much is this going to cost me?" I ask.

 "At least one bottle Old Man.' He says roughly 'but we'll put it on your chit."

 "Thanks Harry," I say fervently.

"Not to worry old boy, if you didn't show up once in a while the whole thing would be a numbing bore."

"Oh! Yeah.' I said, ' I can see how this place, all the booze you can guzzle, lots of sex starved ladies from the cruise ships to roger et al, would be a frightening bore." I wax sarcastic.

"All in a day's work when one's equipped." Harry played along.

"Well, I guess being hung like an ox probably helps." I jabbed.

"How the hell would you know." Harry was just on the edge of angry.

" It's in your file under weapons various." I do the line straight faced. Harry woofs and then roars with laughter.

"I say that is good, may I use it?"

"Of course with my blessing " I make the sign of the cross like the Pope . Harry bows and we both laugh.

"How are you feeling. Nasty night at sea what?" Harry kind of mellows, his voice drops.

"Yeah! What scares me most , I think it's getting easier. The killing I mean, I feel absolutely nothing right now and three people are dead because of me.

Not to mention Jerry." My voice must have echoed the pain. Harry didn't miss a beat.

" Chin, Chin, there Michael. I've killed, its necessary not premeditated in the normal human equation of death for gain. It's war and survival."

"Do you think we will go to hell Harry?"

"Of course ,old boy. Then who the hell would we know anywhere else?" We both laughed then and it felt a little better.

"Never killed a woman before." It was a hard confession.

"Equality, Michael she would have killed you and your friend without remorse. By the by, you have exquisite taste in friends." He meant Cherie and I smiled.

" I do try with some exceptions.' I kid Harry and he laughs again. How much trouble are we in?" I ask.

"Not a lot I think ,although Granny isn't pleased but then he never is. The Governor is a good sort he will take appropriate action. I have a feeling there won't be a lot of relatives looking in on the deceased and if they do we'll want to know all about them."

"You might be surprised. The Chinese have quite a

setup in Panama," I suggested. Harry grunted and I continued.

"Who's Grandma if I might ask or is that need to know?"

"Her name' Harry stated, ' is Elizabeth Aston Helmsworth. From a very rich and prominent London family. Went out to the orient in the twenties to the missions. Unfortunately instead of getting filled up on God, she got full up on General Wang Xuen of the Peoples Liberation Army. Nice chap, they married, no children. However, Elizabeth became an ardent Communist. Back home in England the family was overjoyed." I had to laugh Harry could turn a phrase once in a while.

"Unfortunately, poor old Wang wasn't quite establishment enough and got purged to death." Harry cocked an eyebrow to accent the point. "Elizabeth was thrown in prison for ten years, then released. She still wanted to support the cause. A woman of very deep convictions it seems. The difficulty the regime in Peking had was that she was western and had no relationship to the country. She might be a spy. So they banished her."

"Was she a spy?" I asked.

"No! Well not for us. She lived in Hong Kong so as

to be part of her beloved China. Then Macao until the Porto's got out. I would suspect she was in Taiwan at this point, much to the consternation of the Nationalists. She is a freelance agent but very nasty. She did a lot of damage to our side out in the East. I think old Woodruff used to call her 'Bessy the Hun."

" I for one can appreciate that given what I've seen." I commented.

" She certainly is a catch. I don't know what they can get out of her but I wouldn't put anything past those bastards at Lauret House." The installation Harry mentioned is a rambling estate in the center of jolly old England. Here the combined evils of information extraction has been perfected. I shiver thinking about Au Clair who had been handed over to the gentle ministrations of the clean ,well spoken monsters that inhabit that high tech suction chamber. That mob made the Gestapo look like a girl's choir. I can't say I felt sorry for Bessy. She was far too old for that kind of misuse. However, she would have killed me. How many others had suffered her own playful brand of inquisition.

"How's Pimple doing." I ask.

"Just swimmingly,' said Harry sounding vaguely like Monty Python. No love lost there.

"He won't eat and they have him tied down at the moment. However, I think the boys at the jail are beginning to make inroads." The ex-major's face became hard but I felt nothing for the pimply Toad.

"Did he happen to drop the name of the party or parties behind him?"

"No, he's certain you killed his master and he very much wants you dead. Quite a lot like a faithful dog really. I wonder how he found out you were involved?"

"Everyone in New Orleans knew." I said.

"I see." Harry ruminated.

" Harry someone placed him on the ship and someone knew I would be on it."

"Right, I shall make inquires through the shipping line as to the purchase of tickets and other matters."

"Thanks ." I said off handedly. My mind was elsewhere.

" I wonder if the parties are on the ship?' Harry mussed, 'I'll have a look."

" Make sure you leave my Japanese friend alone." I cautioned.

"Yes, well, the girl ,her father and all that but Winston would like to have a talk with him anyway."

"No, Harry. He would have them killed and I didn't

know what other problems, he could cause us.
Leave that sleeping dog lie."

"Right! Oh! By the by, the brothers Sasha got off
the boat in Puerto Rico."

"Now that is interesting. Wouldn't be that Tilly and
all that lovely money got off at the same place?"

"Yes actually,' Harry laughed low and nasty like
some old horror flick. ' However, by now he's
probably back in Walla Walla or somewhere."

" Probably." I agreed.

"You'll need this by the way' . I removed the post
card with the yellow fish from my pocket and
handed it over. 'What you're looking for is under
the stamp, I think." I added.

"Well I'll be damned.' He laughed, ' where did
you get this."

" Jerry gave it to me for safe keeping. It was in my
compact metal elephant with all the neat little
compartments, along with the gun and some smooth
Irish whiskey.' I paused, ' I hope to God its worth
six lives."

"Jerold wouldn't have moved on it if it weren't"
Said Harry with finality.

"I wish my world could be so black and white."

"I'll drive down with you to Government House

and make sure it goes in the Government Couriers
bag, on my way to the airport."

" Oh! I thought you'd be back on the boat. It's
finished now surely?"

"No ,Jerry was right , Toad was just a pawn. There
is still someone out there that wants me dead and I
don't know why." I hesitated before starting the
next part of my story.

"Also, Jerry wanted me to take a plane ride to New
York in two days."

"Ah yes, the thuggie or whatever.' said Harry
interested, 'I read the report from head office. Rings
with poison in them." I took out the evil looking
gold circle on its chain and handed it to him.

" Quaint, this sort of thing. Lots of secret societies
around especially in the east." Harry held it away
from himself like an unusual snake.

"If these boys are knocking down planes, they
aren't just quaint. Jerry believed the story."

"It's really not our problem you know and Granny
will have your guts for garters if you bugger it up."

"Too much involved for me to walk away."

"What will you do?" Harry asked reasonably.

"Get on the plane, follow him to New York. If he goes to his bank or a show. I meet the ship in the Bahamas. If its something else then I stop it or turn it over to someone who can." The question was could I?

"You'll be out there all by yourself you realize." Harry points out.

"Aren't we always?"

Chapter nine - 1:50 P.m. Between Tortola and
Puerto Rico over the Caribbean Sea.

Lighter Then Air.

I hate airplanes on standard grounds. They are too
heavy to be in midair. My own weight simply
complicates the issue. Further, I really loathe small
planes. They are steady, for the most part but one
feels one's flying on gossamer. There is no net.

The water is deep royal blue below me but it is
ever changing as well. Reefs become lighter areas
on the calm sea. Small unnamed or forgotten islands
dot the surface. Steadily Puerto Rico becomes a
larger green hump on the horizon. Vieques Island
and beyond it Culebra Island sun themselves in the
hazy warmth to our right.

I drive down to the field with Harry making sure
Her Majesty's Diplomatic courier has the post card
in his crested briefcase. We are both couriers, yes
but he golden and I well, Bob's pickup-delivery by
comparison. He, protected by diplomatic and other
immunities and I ,if I live, by God. However, he is a
nice clean faced chap, from a public school with
lovely manners.

Winston, two of his best men , Harry and yours truly follow along to get the clean faced diplomat on his plane. No one's taking any chances. Her Majesty's servant will have added security on the plane. The clean up crew are returning with him. The British Airways plane will only land at Bermuda and home. The passengers are vetted. I watch the fish disappear into the spotless Caribbean sky and wish I were occupying the pouch, in it's stead.

As the little plane hums along, I think of the family. My wife sounds kind of off but is going through her change. She has flashes and such. There are moments when I wonder if she will kill me. I know it's the pittylessness of time catching up with her . I try a lot of small gifts and kisses, these are well received. Late at night when she seems more . her old self she apologizes for being a pain during the day.

I stay home more, as she will jump the kids for small infractions in her chemical imbalance and someone must stand up for them. However, this isn't too often. I am told she is better than many others. Also, taking the part of my prodigy tends to really let her focus anger and frustration on me, which, while it is necessary, hurts a lot.

I read about menopause and offer food ideas to
help. Ever walk into a wood grinder? I leave her to
her own small world. However, I keep trying. Sex
is less interesting for her as she sees herself falling
into lardness . This has an impact, as being human
and male, I too have needs. This fact makes me
more uncomfortable about my little lapse with
Cherie. The kids are now older and aren't around
as much having their own friends. Our
conversations on the phone tend to be shorter and
more abrupt.

It also strikes me that God dealt me a real break
having the wife's mother be a little sick. I cannot
imagine having my lady sprawled on the bathroom
of a cruise cabin naked, drugged and with a gun to
her head or worse still, tossed overboard with my
venerable self.

Of course, I would have said 'kill her', with the
same flippant air, I had tossed Cherie to the
darkness. I would have become Jell-O. Well it
didn't happen, so past and forgotten.

More problems have surfaced, I am told. I
consider them as the big island comes close enough
for us to fly over independent fishing boats out
trying to catch Marlin and such. Sword fish are on
the endangered species list. I no longer order their

steaks when at dinner.

I am embarrassed about destroying the thing that made the Old Man and the Sea my favorite book. I dreamed of being the boy who helped the old man. Changing Papa Hemingway's great story by being in the boat to help kill the great fish and then fight the sharks as they came in drawn by the blood of his passing. Perhaps that is the proper way of men. The book ties all the myths together and makes me yearn for lions along the beach of Africa.

The Cessna dips slightly and I react but it is just an air draft and not the Bermuda Triangle calling.

Harry talks to Marge. She says Jerry's digs have been thoroughly tossed. Wood was removed from the walls. That means the people behind Toad are in front of me or more realistically the Ring Womps have found Jerry's place after the fact. Neither circumstance helps but they are predictable.

I could turn around now and go home but I will not. Perhaps, I owe Jerry and then it's me too. My life is in danger and it will stay that way. I must figure out who and why and stop it.

Also the Swiss ,Avenger of the Ring Womp, has moved his trip up to tomorrow. The tickets are changed. Does he know I'm coming? Has there been some change with respect to the target.

Perhaps more reasonably it's a simple way of identifying if we or others are on to him. New ticket holders or those who also changed their departure date to match his would be a control point. Marge makes sure I have a ticket on the plane under another name. Harry provides me with a nice new British passport in the name of Thomas Alfred, interior decorator. Very humorous!

Phil, the quiet but efficient pilot whose brown competent hands loosely direct the controls, throttles back as we go in to a nice soft dive to the short runway near Yabucoa beneath the Sierra de Cayey. Touchdown is smooth. I find someone who controls his vehicle or plane with one hand, unless its an airbus or big rig, is usually relaxed and confident. I have few worries with Phil, who is a long time friend of Harry's.

I stand beside the plane while Phil retrieves the luggage, including my metal pachyderm. We move across the open field to the small terminal. The single uniformed customs man watches our approach. Phil nods and the man, about thirty thin and wiry, smiles back.

Once we are in the air-conditioning and out of the 84 degree heat, the customs man goes through my

possessions. Phil has nothing. He stops at the
elephant and looks up at me quizzically.
"I really hate my sister-in-law." I smile nastily.
"That should get it done. That's ugly, hombre." He
comments and we exchange conspiratorial smiles
before he tells us to get out of there. We do so in a
rent-a-car, which is positioned just outside.

Highway number three takes you through some
very pretty country. It is tropical green with small
houses, large hotels dot the sea shore to your left
before you enter San Juan, starting up Hwy 26.
From here you can look back over your shoulder
and see the spinal mountains that rise out of the
heart of 'The Beautiful Isle' misty and greenish
blue. Each island in the stream seems to have it's
own kind of beauty. Puerto Rico is Latin: strong but
giving, proud but malleable.

Phil drives but we are both armed. Trying to take
the Saturn from us is going to provide a big surprise
for some 'would be' thief. Yet we are undeterred in
our trip. Phil skirts the Luis Munoz Marin
International Airport and goes directly to the
Crowne Plaza.

The hotel faces on the ocean . Its rooms are
spacious and clean. It is newly renovated having
once been a Holiday Inn.

I wave to Phil, who leaves for his return trip to Tortola as wordlessly as he arrived.

Entering the room I take precautions against intruders securing the two doors. I then strip naked, place the Luger, now completely resurrected from its hiding place in the ugly elephant, under my pillow and sleep until supper.

My body seems rested but I've been through much and my dreams make me wake up periodically. My nerves are fried and I know it.

Finally, I go down and have a light repast at the hotel restaurant. I stick to beef and baked potato. The food is good but I am not in a mood for food and leave more than I eat. The meal is followed by one double Bushmills.

I consider what I am about to do and wonder at my own audacity. I would go swimming but cannot take the chance today, although the water calls me .

Salsa music floats down from the low apartment blocks and tenement three story housing surrounding the street. It is a dark shadowy place but busy. There are people in droves and cars parked nose to tail. Chaotically , automobiles and pedestrians weave past each other like a fiesta. The

women and men exchange looks and sometimes
pair off. The warm night surrounds me, with the
smell of cooking spicy and rich. Laughter, anger,
loud verbal combats and the screams of children, a
cacophony of life. This is how it is lived with gusto
and little worry. I have been all over South America
and everywhere there is poverty. People make their
own fun. They are not connected to the internet.
Their minds are bright and alive. They have nothing
and enjoy life more for it perhaps.

At the corner crouches El Gato Negra a haven for
spies, mercs and other denizens of my world. Sasha
will be there tonight with Legev. I must talk to
them. The Negra is old beyond time with huge wine
barrels and a bar which is always packed. Tourists
and town people do not go here. The police seldom
enter. It is a place where things happen and are not
spoken about. Deals made, countries overthrown,
treasure safaris started, scams hatched and the
death of others contemplated with predictable
results. It is also, by mutual agreement, neutral
ground.

I walk forward aggressively as far away from the

buildings as possible, my eyes directed straight
ahead. To meet other men's eyes is to show
weakness, here that can kill you.

Before me a trash can is overturned. Along with
other unattractive smelly objects are pictures of an
old man and a little girl, the same old man with an
older girl. A younger model of the old man with a
woman who probably was his wife. A pipe extends
from the rubbish. A man's life is gone. No one
seems to want the old man's things. Perhaps they
died before him. Perhaps they lost interest and
moved away to the promise of America. For a
moment I do not want to be old. I do not want to
end up in a home drooling my last days away.
unable to make those around me understand. My
pain will mean nothing. I have seen it. Money and
health are the most important parts of life. No, hope
that is the most important part of life. To be alone is
the worst part. For a moment I almost hope I die
before my wife. To hell with this. I'm getting
maudlin.

I see the two pistalaros siting in the open door and
standing by the fifty -seven Chevy with the
turquoise blue and white two-toned body. The

surface is immaculate and the condition of the car beautiful. The two men, one, a fat black man with a round feeling less face and the other something from Miami Vice, white suit and all. He looks Caucasian and handsome in a swarthy way with blue eyes, surprising in a Latin. He is also suitably unshaved. They are waiting for what or who I wonder? Drugs come to mind. It's none of my business and I pass them by into the smoky belly of El Gato.

Your eyes take a moment to focus in the dark low ceilinged room. A long faced pistalaro at the bar reacts to me like I am made of gold. The Puerto Rican is waiting for little old me. He now makes as if I am the least important thing in the universe. I pass, ignoring him, ignoring me. Perhaps he is CIA but I doubt it gravely. He certainly isn't a Ring Womp not in that cheesy suit. I wonder in a half second if he has relatives outside? I glance at his rat like thin Mexican bandito face with the lush mustachio and the long side burns. His rich brown eyes are clear and calculating. Under his coat bulges a magnum, why am I not surprised?

Sasha is at a table at the end of the bar. The ex-

KGB man faces the door, good basic tactics. Legev is by the end of the bar. I get a passing glance from him. Sasha is in deep conversation with a very competent looking Eastern European type. The shoes are better than before the fall of the 'Evil Empire' but the taste in clothing still leaves something to be desired, at least in this case. A dark suit in this climate is for drug dealers and non islanders. I wear a champagne beige Frasers suit, a white short sleeved shirt with a yellow tie dotted with blue and gold gothic flower designs. The suit looks like the man wearing it has money or better represents it..

The East Euro finishes his conversation, stands, his belly extends appropriately over his belt and walks past me like a buffalo. Others clear a path, if that says anything. He has a scar, I notice, that starts at his temple and extends in a white river to his chin . The eyes are cold but there seems to be a spark of intelligence. If I were Sasha I would hire the bloke who gave him the scar but then it's not my problem.

I walk over to the table and smile non aggressively. "The Coca Cola salesman' I suggest and look over at the Pepsi fountain behind the bar. 'developing new business?" It takes him a moment then he tags me from the ship.

" The tourist who almost missed the ship.' He smiles nastily or perhaps that's the only way he can smile.

" May I buy you a drink?" I offer. Legev stands at the bar behind me. I know because Sasha makes a small hand movement to warn him off ,for the moment.

"But of course, my friend." He says. His hand automatically moves below the table.

"Let us keep our hands above the table shall we?" I suggest. Sasha's smile disappears and the real man emerges for a moment. Primal, physical, brutality in his hatchet face impacts heavily on the Psyche. Have I looked like that? Lord help me, probably. 'I mean you no harm.' I continue,' and I have a proposition, which may be of interest."

The face changes again. A deal, Russians love to deal. It gives them a point from which to double cross you. That is not fair either, not all Russians but this one, oh yes.

I sit placing my hat on the table and wave to a passing waiter.

"Si Senor" Says the little man. I gester to Sasha for his order.

" Brandy, Napoleon ." He says.

" Bacardi and Lime,. Por favor?.' I finish.'

"The man nods and wanders off.'

Both of Sasha's hands are on the table now.
Legev has probably got me covered. I sit with my
side to the door. This allows for less of a target and
does not expose my back.

"You have a proposition." He says cutting to the chase

" Perhaps for the right individual.' I smile. He says
nothing waiting now.

" Let us say on a ship, items of value were
exchanged. A post card with certain information
and a bag containing, say for discussion sake,' I
throw off, 'A million Cayman.' I have his
undivided attention . He knows this and I know he
knows it. Sasha is waiting hungrily for the next part.
'One of the items may have become lost."

"Really that would be a very difficult trick my
friend." Sasha is wondering which item. He thinks
he knows where the money is. Which means Tilly
and his entourage are still on the island.. As an
independent, he isn't taking on the Chinese, that
would be suicide. Tilly and his group of beefy
security guards are a much easier target."

"Which item or am I to guess?" He snaps off.
"The card."
"Only a very brave or stupid man would have that."
He knows as I do that the Chinese will hunt down
the thief or thieves unless they have agency
protection. He is probing.

"I noticed that you seemed to have sufficient
personnel on the ship, to be effective."
I ignored the probe.
He sneaks a look at Leveg and his face gets hard. I
know more then he does and that makes me
dangerous."
"If it makes you happy."
"The three of you should be equal to the job." I nod
to myself.

"I think you're mistaken." he reacts folding back
into himself..

"You, Leveg and the other one." I say off
handedly. Then hesitate. ' Maybe my proposition is
not relevant if you're undermanned". He seems to
realize what I am talking about. It is obvious he
wants to hear the deal.
"The other, on the ship, is 'in house' but we have
resources." He says very delicately.
"Fine,' I say considering whether I should offer or

not. Then I nod as if I have made up my mind. 'If you could lay your hands on the money. Then my people are willing to provide the first object for say $750,000.00 US. This would involve a cleared path from the original purchasers.' I have offered him a great deal for a small amount.' Not only will he have $500,000.00 US in hand. The information on the card is worth far in excess of that. The Russians would pay substantially. The Japanese more still. I have also suggested that the Chinese will not hunt him down, he might resell the item to them."

"It is also possible that you are looking for a target for the original purchasers." He says way ahead of me.

" Then you are not interested. I understand. " Our drinks come and there is a moment of silence.

" Who are your people?" He demands

" An interested party, if you come by the money we will see. If not the offer is redundant." I leave money on the table.

' How will I contact you?"

" I will contact you." I say rising to leave the glass untouched.

I head for the door. Rat face is on a different stool

which means he has been outside, fine we will see.
I think I know now who killed Jerry, who is trying
to kill me and why seven men died just after the Bay
of Pigs. Strangely at this point the old folks home
looks pretty good.

Chapter ten - 8:30 A.m., St. Luis de Los Palma St.,
San Juan, Puerto Rico

A Moment Of Truth.

As I walk toward the street door of El Gato, the
rat-like pistolero stands and follows. What is about
to occur will come down to fear and how I handle i
My training, such as it is, will be a factor and luck.

These guys are not Ring Womps. If the European
assassins league knew who I was, the local
authorities would find me under a truck. A nice
provable accident. No, this was going to be messy.
These people could be police but I cannot believe
San Juan's finest are lead by this chump. No, I
figure the man behind Toad, is also behind these
clowns. They are a back stop. The figure behind the
problem does not think I will show up here but
leaves these guys on guard, just in case. They are
cheap insurance and will only get the bulk of their
money if I show up. Then they must either obtain
my esteemed person or kill same. It is my intent tha
they go away poor.

I exit the door and turn right walking away from
the entrance quickly but not running. The intent on
my part is to put some space between me and the
door before Rat Face comes out and choreographs

my demise. I am quite a few cars lengths away
before his appearance. I watch him in the mirror
flap of my sun glasses. These adjust just fine to
night vision and have a number of options, this is
one.

As I suspect he hails Fat Boy and Miami Vice.
Increasing my speed slightly, I watch as he removes
the magnum from his belt. There is no holster,
which confirms my belief that these man are not the
local constabulary. The other two come forward on
the street side of the cars, guns drawn.

My next move is also calculated. A quick duck
between the cars stops all of them for a moment.
This allows me to remove the Luger from my ankle
holster, a gift from Harry. The silencer is hidden at
the small of my back and attaches in seconds. I
move to the street side of the Buick which is
providing my cover. Reaching around the fender
pointing the Luger back toward Fat Boy and Miami
Vice who are coming to intercept me. I brace my
arm along the side of the car and target the bulk of
Fat Boy's body. In a situation like this you hit what
you aim at. A wayward bullet does not know the
good guys from the bad and I will buy the farm
before some kid does in my place. I squeeze the
trigger like they taught me at good old spy school.
There is the soft whoosh as the Luger works

flawlessly. Fat Boy takes the nine millimeter slug chest high and goes down like a sack of cement. He does not get up. Miami Vice ducks behind the car he is next to Rat Face finds the engine of a second vehicle to hide behind. This momentary lapse lets me use a passing truck to slip across the narrow street. I disappear between two cars and finally cross ten feet of empty lot, to an abandoned Chrysler. The car's bulk allows for a momentary hiding place. Normally I would have just plain run. In this case underestimating the opposition could be fatal.

While the fact that Fat Boy had a silencer removed any possibility of him being a police officer, it did bring out the point that these sewer dwellers might be a lot better than I thought and made me change my plan.

The question was how much did my friends want me? An unsuspecting target who is unarmed is one thing . A thinking enemy ready to use his weapon is a totally different ballpark. Under normal circumstances, I would have expected the opposition to see good old Fat Boy take the fall and make for the hills. Because in a minute ,wait for it, a pretty girl in a blue dress sees Fat Boy and screams. People are either drawn to his body or run for it, more in the latter group. Someone should drop a dime now and the police should be on their way. It will depend upon traffic and other conditions when they will arrive.

The two remaining pistoleros split up and come after me. They ignore the crowd around Fat Boy and come to the street side of the row of cars only a few feet away. Rat Face is farther up the street toward El Gato. Miami Vice is closer to me. Both duck down and search the lot in its half darkness for their quarry. The payoff for this one must be high, very high. These two understood what they were taking on, no questions asked. So it is kill or be killed.

Rat face and Miami Vice yell back and forth. I figure they think I have made a run for it.
I am Japed down behind the engine which is the only thing that will stop a bullet on a car with any consistency. I have seen a thirty-eight fired through a car door, the bullet being stopped by the window glass but these two are using much heavier artillery.

The next move must be tactical. They figure I have run. At least that is what they are saying perhaps thinking the stupid Gringo does not understand. I hear Rat Face flank me up the lot but far enough away not to worry about at this moment.

Miami Vice is about to make a major tactical blunder. He enters the space between a Concord and a Ford truck . He waits. I think my attention is being held by his position so that Rat Face can take me from behind. However, he has to find me and I have the night vision glasses. Miami Vice spins out to point his gun up the line of cars away from me however he is too small a target. I wait. Crossing my thumbs over the back of the Luger, I tighten my two hand grip. He hesitates then spins out the other way. This gives me the most of his body at about15 feet. I squeeze the trigger the bullet catches Miami Vice in the lower waist. It is then I notice the thin armor he is wearing edging out from under his colored shirt. I fire again this time below the armor into his belly and intestines . He screams and roles back against the car. This offers me his chest. I fire once more. The bullet goes through his throat and breaks a car window on the other side of the street. No one else is harmed thank God but Miami is done.

I know I have wasted far too much time in this position . I instantly spin and move toward the next car that is junked a few feet behind the first. My bulky body is a good target; too good. I see the flash of Rat Face's gun. He has not cut the wad in the shells. A finger of flame extends almost a foot, rocking him in his stance. The finger points satanically at me. A 44 load hits on an angle and spins me like a top. I go down, there is an agony in my chest that no pill is going to remove. At first I feel nothing but in moments the pain streaks

through me like molten fire. I have not dropped the
Luger . I grip it and scramble the remaining two feet
to flop behind the safety of a second junker. Rat
Face's second bullet blasts a hole in the metal above
my head. Large guns fired over more than 20 feet
are hard to target. They tend to jump, screwing up
the shot, unless the shooter knows his weapon well
and can control it

My hand comes away from my chest covered with
blood. I am not sure how bad it is but it isn't
superficial. The fact that I can still breath and do not
have a sucking sound coming from my chest tells
me the lung is still operating. I will not speak for
any of my other anatomy. My mind settles slightly. I
know I have to kill him fast. Whatever happens
now, the pistolero has to come to me. He isn't sure
I'm dead which means I have to move. The pain of
this action is spectacular. Initially, I try to rise but
decide crawling is better. I make the other end of the
old Chevy and hide in the grass slightly beyond it.
The light from the street shines on and through
holes in the ancient Pontiac, Rat Face is using for
cover. I see movement. He is crawling up to my end
of the car. Unaware of my night vision glasses
which have stayed on. He places himself before a
large hole in the rusted metal. I aim at the center of
his moving body and fire three more times. He rolls
away as the first slug hits him. This allows the

second and the third to find their mark as well. The
pistolero falls away from me on his back. He isn't
dead but he isn't going anywhere either. If he does I
will kill him. If I can stay awake!

The voice is light as air and soft as a feather.

" I believe we are going to have rain." This of
course is the phrase of the day. Only Marg would
know it and be there. She would have had to follow
me. I had not sensed her. Which made her very
good or me getting soft.

"Its best to have an umbrella then." I gasp into the
darkness. It might be someone else. I redirect my
Luger to cover the general direction.

"If one is available.' Marg finishes the phrase.
'How bad are you?" she says as if considering what
to do.

" I am shot up but I don't think I'll die." I try to use
my hanky to stop the flow of blood.

"Right , I'm going to pass you. So don't shoot me."
Her lithe body materialized out of the darkness and
leaps over me like a deer. I get the faint odor of
lavender in her passing. She continues moving in a
zigzag pattern toward the car where Rat Face is
hidden, cursing in Spanish. She reaches the nose of
the Pontiac. With one simple swinging motion she
brings her Beretta to bare on Rat Face and fires
twice, short sharp barks. She then removes

something from her pocket, moves over to the dead pistolero and empties a white powder all over him. I presume it is cocaine. It has become part of the kit of late, as it offers an excellent dodge. The police will figure this is a drug trade gone bad and be less interested. Rat face and his companions should have yellow sheets to get to Oz on.

Marg sprints back as the sirens increase in volume. Her hand touches my rib cage by mistake and I scream into her shoulder. I partially black out the pain is so great. Maybe this is it, I think groggily. I can feel everything. If you're dying you can't feel your outer extremities. Isn't that the indicator.

"Good God!' she says in exasperation.' I'll try to lift you but if you can't stay up, I will have to leave you here for the police. They won't be kind but you'll get medical care."

"I can make it,' I say with bravado. 'Marg is surpassingly strong. She somehow gets my two hundred pounds off the ground and on my feet which take the load. I make myself move from pure mean mindedness, because that's all there is left. The trip across a second lot which connects to the first on an angle and opens onto a second street is long and excruciating. I fall once but Marg puts her shoulder under me and gets me the last few feet to the car. Marg opens the Toyota holding me up. I fall

into the seat and relax. Holding the wound where
the blood seems to be coagulating in the dim light
of the interior. Marg sprays the outside of the car
and the ground leading to it. This canned concoction
is a combination of various blood types. It will be
impossible for the opposition to identify my blood.
It also has a detergent which will dissolve the blood
on the car in a few minutes.

The first police jeep rounds the corner as Marg
gets into the car. We wait as it passes.

"Do you have any booze?" I ask.

"What!" she returns taken aback by the question.

"Whiskey." I clarify.

She opens the glove compartment and hands me a
mickey of Seagram's VO . I open it, take a swig,
then pour the remainder on the wound, howl like a
banshee and immediately pass out.

Chapter eleven - 9:30 A safe house, somewhere in
San Juan, Puerto Rico.

A Girl With Lion Eyes

I remember very little of arriving at the safe
house. Vaguely, the climb of a few steps, the
dramatic pain and Marg's persistent voice
demanding that I not fall down or black out. I
concentrate on the voice and move along as best I
can. My thoughts are polluted like a dream, during
illness. The voice urging me on, is worn out,
drained by a great struggle getting me to the bed
through the small four room cottage. I hit the bed
and lay completely still. I could hear my own
breathing and realized that I was still alive. My
mouth was dry and a child's voice, I remember that
voice from long ago, asks for water. The corn
coloured head on the pillow beside me does not
move. The wife will go in a minute, it always takes
her time to get up. My mind leaves on vacant
voyages but the pain brings me back . Someone,
me! starts to moan piteously. The blond head has
disappeared. In a moment I look into Lion Eyes.
Golden orbs touched with spots of black and brown,
slightly cross but kind and caring.
I am stripped of my saturated shirt and jacket
against my protest. A no nonsense voice tells me to

shut up and get a spine. After that, I start to get a grip and stoically help the girl with the lion eyes, who seems to want to help me. I am cleaned and bandaged with calculated efficiency.

Marg is a nurse, I now remember reading somewhere. She gets me to take some Tylenol-threes and leaves me. The water tastes good and I seem to be alright if I don't move too much. Then suddenly a fall into an abyss of black nothingness.

Coming to, I watch as she gives me a big syringe of what must be a pain killer or antibiotic in the left arm. I realize, in a faraway haze, my body is naked. Lion Eyes covers my sweat drenched form with a light blanket and I sleep again. I have a fever which makes me slide in and out of conscious thought. On one occasion I am very cold, my body shakes and my teeth chatter. Lion Eyes, turns off the air conditioning. She strips off her black body suit and moments later slips naked into the bed, wrapping her warm body around my shaking form. I hold her like a drowning man. The smell of lavender surrounds me and makes me think of far away and long ago when my aunt used to take care of me. Lavender was her trademark scent. The ancient smell somehow calms me. In making me think of that faraway , better time the chills diminish

I continue to wake up but the pain seems to have
lessened and my mind to clear. I seem to be getting
better. I concentrate my mind on the moment. I
demand that my body remain under control, it does.
I have been taught that the mind is only one third in
operation at any given time. By focusing my mind
on one point and continually demanding whatever
you want to happen, it usually does. In the case of
the body, it is a form of self hypnosis. Finally the
fever breaks and I sleep.

The clock tells me its three in the morning. The
sleep is deep and refreshing when I awake it is dark.
I am disoriented until I feel my wife next to me. Her
soft body is naked. I spoon to her, my stomach to
her cold bum. I move softly against her, she
grumbles in her sleep then seems to stiffen. I push
my body against her. I am aroused. Perhaps it is
being alive or perhaps it does not happen, perhaps it
is a dream. I find the spot below her full behind and
push softly she raises her leg to rest on mine
increasing my window of opportunity and allowing
me to slide in. She makes a little moaning sound. I
move forward again then slowly back and forth
while my hands pet her body messaging her breast
with one hand rubbing her neck with the other.
She opens to me as if reluctantly but I am in. Now
because I hurt, I slowly make love to her. Slowly,

forever, until as I slide along the edge of the blade
of sexual completion. I push against her hard,
compacting her bum cheeks, making her gasp,
empty myself. At the same time the pain runs
through my chest but it is bearable. I finish, tell her I
love her, in a strange slurred voice which I hardly
recognize, then sleep without further adieu.

Light comes through the window. I am alone in
the bed. My mind is clear although that seems
suspect. The wound is bright with white bandage
look around the plain little house. The woman w
stands naked by the little stove in the next room is
completely ignorant of my stare. Whatever she is
making smells mouthwatering .I detect chicken. Her
body is comfortable in the nude. Marg is about
thirty two. With the exception of slightly enhanced
hips, she has a lovely body. Her shoulder length hair
lies on soft white expanses that are lean and look
muscular. This seems to continue down her back to
her tight round buttocks and dancer's legs. The feet
are ugly, multi-veined and large. She seems to
become aware of my evaluation and turns to face
me. There is no false modesty. Small pointed
breasts signal me out. Her tummy is a petit, soft
pillow and below, well, she is a blond.

Her eyes draw the viewer from other pursuits to
her face. I have never seen golden eyes before. They

are lustrous and demand attention. They hypnotize and unconsciously make a man want to have their whole attention. She places the soup carefully in a bowl and carries a small white wicker tray over to me. She helps me sit up. This hurts but is not outside my control. Placing a towel over my chest she hands me a spoon.

"You're capable of feeding yourself." she says a little roughly. I smile. Her face is longer than I would have expected. Her nose is a sharp triangle above full lips and a generous smile. However the leanness of the face also stipulates a certain craftiness. That makes the watcher recalculate his immediate reaction.

"I guess I owe you a lot. Thanks!" Her face seems to sneer.

" As soon as you can, you're going home. Granny demands it. Quote, our fearless leader 'I can't afford anymore people, get him out of there.' She stops for a moment and plays with the next bit. 'He said I could kill you, if you were any trouble.. I should suspect he was having a bad day." Her smile is bright and gracious.

"When's the plane today? I ask spooning a little of the chicken soup into my mouth and allowing it to trickle down my famished throat. It is the best soup I have ever tasted. Lord its the best soup anyone has ever made. I consider Utah and bigamy but shelve the idea. Her nude body demands action on my part which I couldn't hope to complete. I am also questioning my dream of last night and if it happened. I get a real chill and change the subject.

"Was there anything in the newspaper about last night,"

"I haven't had a lot of time to look. She smiles uncoils her lithe body and moves toward the door. Her body moves with that sweet perfect rhythm of women. I love to watch. Marg seems to be completely undisturbed by her nudity, not knowing seemingly the impact it's having on me.

"If you're going out like that this street is lucky indeed." I tease. She laughs softly

"Not likely," she retorts. As if on cue she puts a short white velveteen cover on and ties the belt in the front. Then, with one simple move, she opens the door and grabs the paper from the mail box. Then closes off our little world again.

Having acquired the local rag, Marg moves to the table and looks through it. About half way on she stops and peruses the Spanish.

"It says here that three known criminals were killed in a gun battle with what police describe as a rival gang. ' Marg's face hardens 'Would you mind telling me, who those men were and why you had to kill them?"

"I didn't choose the job or the place. I stopped in to see Sasha at El Gato. He was on the ship and I thought I might get some information from him."
"Did You?" she asks.
" Yes, I think I know who killed Jerry. I also think that individual is trying to kill me."
"Those ring people.?" She asks folding her arms.
"No, oh they would have but they didn't know about Jerry.."
" The wood they pulled off the wall, was that somewhere important? Covering stuff that Jerry would have hidden there? Was it firm business.?"
"Yes, old codes. Sometimes they resurrect them for short periods or to send misinformation."

"Was that the only place where they went into the wall?"

" They trashed the place."

" Whoever did it was firm or at least has the basic information to make the selection. They have to be agency. That's not Ring Womps."

"Then who?" she demands. The golden windows get dark with frustration.

"Look, as long as I'm alive, I'm a problem for this person. That is why he will track me down. He has very little sophistication in high tech surveillance or perhaps not a great availability to acquire it on short notice.. He knew, however, I was going to be on the island. He's monitoring your messages.

"That's not possible." Marg protested but we both knew anything is possible.

" I don't know how they're doing it. Don't call in or go home for two days minimum. Stay in touch with Granny but use the back up channels ."

"You stay here and I will see to it you leave safely." She promised.

"Neither of us are safe. None of us out here are safe and I say that with no exceptions."

"I have to be on that plane for two reasons. One, it will screw up his thinking. Two, Jerry asked me to. There might be a lot of people who will die if I don't go there and make sure."

"Your completely potty. You won't make it to the airport let alone on the plane. What if you start to bleed again? I suppose I could go with you."

"No you can't. The two of us is what he is expecting. Listen how bad is this thing really?" I ask.

"I am no doctor." She qualifies.

"Most doctors would be standing around sucking there thumbs without good nurses.' She smiles. 'Then gets very cold and honest.

"The forty four caliber bullet caught you across the chest. Then burrowed into your side between two ribs and stripped most of the flesh from them. In the end it tore up your chest muscles on the left side and exited."

"So its basically superficial." I ask.

"No, it is bloody well not. I put a number of stitches in the wound and the wadding is holding the rest together.

Going to the bathroom is one thing, you might get that done by yourself. Going to the airport, wandering around, making your contact with all the tension that initiates; maybe but more likely you'd blackout or lose your direction.

Let's say you actually get on the plane with this villein. You have to be ready to meet him and kill him. One punch to your ribs and you'd be less then useless. No it's impossible."

" If you pick up a paper tomorrow and a plane with three hundred people goes into the drink then what?"

"We'll be nice and safe here."

"That's why I have to go. Listen if the guy goes to his bank or sees his aunt, that's it. "

" You have to follow him you didn't pick me up all over town. Don't you think he'll have backup?"

"Oh I knew you were there but you didn't give off bad vibes."

"What?" she demands. Wondering no doubt if I'm into Voodoo or something.

"You didn't make me twitch. You know if the enemy is following or not after a while. You weren't a threat, therefor no reaction. As a matter of fact I would have been surprised if you hadn't showed up. As to him I'm pretty good at what I do."

"You need eight people for a proper surveillance." she interrupted.

"It won't take overnight. This will happen within three hours after he gets off the plane." That was the time sequence for the others but it's hard to say if he had anything to do with it. One of the planes had nothing to do with him." I lay back and weigh my strength against the problem and decided I can do it.

"Who is trying to kill you or don't I get to know?"

"No, because right now I have a theory not proof."

"Share your theory.." she said sitting on the end of the bed pulling her knees up under her chin thereby showing off everything else she owned. I decided to tell her some of it.

"Jerry hesitated. That's why he died. No more then a second but it was fatal."

" Why! "she asked.

" Whoever came through the door was out of the

ordinary." I stopped, 'If it had been a waiter or
something he would have never let him in. Whoever
it was knew the correct knock and the phrase of the
day. He was Firm or knew the waltz. That my love,
is what makes him extremely dangerous. I think we
all know him and trust him." At first I thought it
might be you but you were here. Don't trust anyone
and I mean it."

"It could have been you." her voice drops and
becomes dangerous.

"I was in the dinning room, you can ask Harry, he
checked it out." It disturbed me that he would but
then the prime directive was to make sure.

"I can't.' She says as if hesitant to continue.
'Someone shot him."

"What!' I hear her but cannot believe I do so. 'Is he
dead? When the hell did this happen?"

"Last Night, they shot Harry and a warder at the
jail in Road Town. Your friend Toad is dead too.
I think Harry was nervous about the situation and
went to check. He must have walked right in on it.
The Chinese woman was suffocated with a pillow in
the hospital."

Jesus! Harry dead. I had just seen him the day
before. Maybe they were going to try to hang this
one on me. Marg would be following me for a

reason and had inadvertently cleared me. Of course, I could have an accomplice and so Granny was listening for the outcome from San Juan. I never think of myself as a risk. Now I had to take this into account.

The pain of Harry's loss was great. I had few friends spys seldom do. I would miss his wolf laugh and his dogged friendship. I close his file though, like so many others, like Jerry's. Sentimentality will get you killed but I promised myself I would get even. I never make threats, I make promises and keep them.

"'What did you get from Sasha?"

"There was someone else on the ship. Someone who is 'in house'. That means he is KGB or Russian Internal Security which is the same thing."

"Maybe he meant your pimply friend." she suggests.

"The KGB might use someone like good old pimple back in Mother Russia for rough stuff but not out here. He has no finesse and less intelligence. Anyway the Russians have become a lot more sophisticated. The reason people like Sasha and Legev are working on their own, is that they got rid of the worst elements of the old school.

"So its a mole then." Her voice dropped.
"Maybe , but I think something much more intricate."

Chapter twelve - 5:30 Pm, Luis Munoz Martin
International Airport, San Juan, Puerto Rico.

An Uplifting Experience.

All airports are the same. A flow of people trying
to find their planes, relatives or luggage. The latter
of which is on its way to Kuala Lumpur. Bright
shiny, store fronts selling souvenirs, books, disks
and other items to make the trip shorter. In San Juan
the voices were primarily Spanish. However, the
cacophony which is the normal mix of the United
Nations is present. English and Spanish information
is sent over hidden speakers interrupting elevator
music. Monitors flickered with flight changes
arrivals and departures.

Today I was to 'Fly The Friendly Sky's,' of
United Airlines to New York. The 747 is going to
be crowded. Three hundred people seemed to be
sitting in the area around the debarkation port. I
hobble in on my copper coloured cane with its
squarish brown plastic handle. In part the cane is a
prop, in part it holds my wounded body up. It also
contains a thirty- two caliber plastic gun, which
fires from the front end of the tubular hand grip.
The pain is intense. I drag myself to a seat. While

sweating heavily, I haven't blacked out which is at least something.

Marg gives me hell for most of the day. When she realizes I am going no matter what, she becomes accepting of the situation. Lion Eyes rebinds my wounds, then gives me as much pain killer as possible without having me go to sleep. The cane is a present along with a large leather brief case with a wide strap from home office. This is provided to hold cloth samples and diagrams of rooms to be decorated. I also get a cad disc for my lap top. This is so, I can play with colours for various rooms as defined by the sketches, in keeping with my cover. All of this had been sent in over by Special Services Department. Joy!

The Swiss Ring Womp comes in late. He walks like he is God or a close relative. I watch him scan the crowd without doing it. He's good! I in turn watch him while not doing it. I hope I do so as well as he. My drawings are spread on my lap for perusal. I make non-notes in keeping with the cover. This time I don't look for a women and child or some other cover. This animal is of a different stripe. I am unsure what will happen if he twigs to me. The Womp picks a seat some distance away and opens a New York Times, which he now reads completely oblivious to the rest of the waiters.

es and

At first glance the face is cold, almost brittle.
There is something close to primal in it. He might
be German but no German face ever had cheek
bones like that. There is a very French cast to the
bone structure. A kind of hardman Francais,. you
might see on the docks of Bordeau or in the quarter
of Paris. The hair is short and blond, above a
squarish forehead. Thin brows come close together
as he reads. This seems to be an indication of
increased concentration. A short Nordic nose is
supported by a hard thin mouth and a dimpled chin.

This is the kind of face that you don't come into
contact with unless you want real trouble. There is a
raw dynamic to the man. Women will probably fall
for the cruel, saber blue eyes, his broad shoulders
and weight lifters, thirty something body.

As an opponent he would be fast, very competent
and instantly lethal. He has no suggestion of
arrogance which makes a man vulnerable. In the
end, death would be business and delt in that
manner.

His panther like body is dressed in tan pants and
an open neck, white Polo shirt. This allows for the
glimmer of gold chain, leading no doubt to the
brother of the ring I carry in my pocket. Covering
the rest is an expensive leather, circa nineteen
forties fighter pilot's jacket. He wares an expensive
Jaeger-LeCoultre watch which glimmers above a

gold wrist chain.

The flight is called, people rush to be in line first.. The Ring Womp stands slowly. He obtains his carry on bag from the seat next to him and watches the flow. Placing my drawings into the pouch, I rise on my cane with gritted teeth, against the pain. I adjust the glasses which are also part of my get up. Dressed in gray pants and a blue sports jacket with silver buttons, chosen by Marg, I seem to fit in. The shirt is white and open. My glasses are slightly magnified to actually help with close up reading. At least the people in Special Services are trying. I hobble slowly toward the departure gate then stop to lean on the end of a bench to rest. The majority of passengers move forward in a pushing throng. The Womp slides into the flow, I follow.

Passenger planes are basically large buses. The smell, while neutral, still has the musty odor of use. I sit and turn my television on to see what the in-flight movie will be. The Ring Womp sits about twelve rows ahead of me and disappears into his Times.

I waited until we were off the ground then lay out to sleep. It was a calculated risk . I didn't think he would try to kill me on the plane. After all he shouldn't know me. Also, I would need all my strength for what was ahead.

NewYork is huge. It seems to spread like an
amoebae eating up the surrounding county side. The
tall sky scrapers which are its signature are partially
covered in mist. Rain falls below us as we break
through the overhead and descend to Laguardia.
There is a tremor as the big jet, having circled for
fifteen minutes, now fights cross winds. I am as
awake as possible and the pain killers are slowly
coming out so I am raw nerved as well. I play with
my cad system. The guy next to me, who sells
siding, informs me that he also has the ability to
change colours on his programs. This allows him to
use various houses for demonstration purposes.
Having spoken to him kindly, I get a complete
education on siding, including the fact that wood
siding had now been perfected. I absorb the
information as best I can. The Womp only leaves
his seat to go to the bathroom. I wait till later and
use the same facility scanning it to make sure he
hasn't left some cute little package behind.

Now as we drop down the old Ring Womp
tightens up. He becomes more watchful. I in turn
continue my conversation with the siding guy. He is
a Bush supporter. I am not. I figure he will be
controlled in great part by his father. I believe his
primary plan is to have an America built on
Canadian resources and cheap Mexican labour all

under the same roof. Everybody gets American citizenship. No thank you, very much.

The outcome may not be that important anyway. In a place called Davos, in Switzerland, the world's hundred largest corporations had a little party. A decree was sent out to world leaders, the media and just about anyone with any power or mattered to attend. The Corporate boys then sat down and decided where the world was going in the near future with little if any help from the participants. The politicians came, even the President of these United States, with all that money concentrated in one place, I wonder why? Well, governments can't control money. It moves with the speed of light. They cannot dictate to it, so they must accept its primacy and the will of those who wield its power. I figured the west was reasonably safe. You see, they need democracy or at least freedom to operate, make deals and so on. I remember though, that the largest corporations in the world, made money in Nazi Germany using slave labour in the thirties. The truly powerful must always be watched or you will pay the price every time. Corporations as a rule are set up to make as much money as possible, period. Those who get in the way beware.

The plane hit the tarmac with a hiss. Then trundled over to the arrival connector. I watch for

the Womp to leave, he takes his time, as do I.
Figuring out which aisle he will use I stand up
directly in front of him. Then slowly painfully, its
real by the way, lumber down the isle before him.
At the end of the aisle, I move over and offer to
allow him to pass me, apologizing for holding him
up. Being Swiss he is polite and says not to worry,
so I continue and he follows. His voice is metallic.
There is nothing human about this bird.

  We go through customs together. My cane is
placed on the outside of the metal detector it is light
and so not considered a potential weapon. Now out
into the mist of the New York traffic, a jostling
pushing hoard, oblivious to my cane . I set my
shoulders and plow through having been here
before. The Womp has moved off to the right. I
follow him down the corridor, keeping an eye on his
head as he disappears into a convenient door. This
portal should lead into the center of the airport and
should be closed. I place my bag on a bench. Slip
the plastic United Airlines name plate onto my
pocket and place a plastic identification card with
my picture on it around my neck. Moving to the
door I take out an electronic key which enters the
lock. Showing small light pattern changes from the
array of light bulbs on its side, while it negotiates
the lock and finally opens it. I am through. The
corridor is

long and empty. My heat sensor indicated the
direction of target. I have identified the Womp's
heat signature while slowly moving down the aisle
before him. This signature should take me right to
him without being too close. I move out as quickly
as possible. The small green light tells me the way,
a red light indicates I go off track. My journey takes
me past masses of offices, a large cafeteria and
finally into the baggage control area. Thousands of
pieces of luggage move around me being miss-
handled by the swearing workers. I see him ahead of
me now as he moves across the air port areas. In the
moments difference between my losing sight of him
and him entering the empty corridor he has donned
a gray set of Luftliepzig coveralls.

Luftliepzig was a small private airline for senior
members of the East German Government. The
name was new. The jets flown by this efficient and
safe little operation would normally have been
absorbed by the major German carrier on unification
but some intelligent bureaucrat had purchased it.
While the principles haggled over the price it had
grown conservatively over the past ten years into a
profitable overseas carrier for the general public
much to the German Government's discomfort.

Thirty minutes later I arrive at the Luftliepzig
hanger. The planes inside were waiting quietly for

their call into the cool spring skies of New York. Interestingly enough, on entering, I realize no one is in the great hanger. If that is not suspicious I don't know what is. Two air buses sit next to each other gleaming in the florescent light.

I am too late. The Womp, who had a good head start, has had almost half an hour in the hanger before my arrival. What has he done in that time? Is he still here. Perhaps this isn't his last stop?

I enter the hanger gingerly moving toward the planes. I will call the authorities. That's all I can do now, I think bitterly. Then I look down at the heat seeker and realize I am not alone. The hunter has become the hunted.

My turn is just enough to bring me face to face with the Womp, who has moved silently up behind me. I hold the cane toward him and wait.

"Heat signature bien, very good.' His computer like voice irritates, 'You are secret service Englais yes?" He smiles cold bloodedly. 'You will have the ring eh? All my work and you come to me." he laughed and I didn't like it. I should just kill him . Was it that easy? Was I him?

"Don't move." I breath out and direct the cane at him. He stops considering the handle.

"Poison dart perhaps, bien." he smiles. 'The question, mon amis, is which plane? If you kill me then how many die, eh?" The question was a good one.

"Perhaps, neither of these planes eh? Perhaps, another eh?"

"Perhaps, I will allow the police to work that out." I say in French.

"Canadian Francais, merd, that is droll. You will not live to tell the police." The move was faster then I could have ever expected. I pulled the trigger on the plastic gun and nothing. In the next instant he was on me.

The Womp's right hand shot out to impact on the center of my chest. Two things save me from the karate blow that would have stopped my heart. One I kick out at him using the useless cane as a support. This action turns my body to the right and allows him to snap one of my ribs, on the side of my body opposite the bullet wound. My foot connects with his pelvis. I'm a little high, in a real fight you never hit what you're aiming at. However, I am close enough to stop him for a moment. My pain is intense but I still swing first and connect with the back of his head . He is moving so its a glancing blow but enough to stagger him . I back away and try the cane again, nothing. I curse the Special Services Department and all those whoever developed the plastic gun, hidden in the handle. He moves in for the kill. I try a second kick. Bad mistake, he drops and swings his leg like a cycle knocking my planted leg out from under me and placing me on my back. He is up and on me in an instant. We grapple, his hands close on my throat and the pressure is terrific. I feel my life being closed off like a faucet. The air is being cut but the blind panic that should set in doesn't. This is where training comes in . He has left my hands free. I chop him across the bridge of the nose. This causes uncalculated pain, a flow of blood and stuns him. I drive the palm of my right hand at the point of his nose, with the purpose of driving the now broken bone at the top his nose, back into his brain. He moves up and to the right and I miss but his hands loosen. I drive my fist into his now visible crotch. He lets out a scream and I heave him off my body

The Womp stands off breathing deeply, his eyes flash with cold fury, his face a mask of hatred. He hesitates for only a moment then dives. I grab the cane but have it crushed between us as we fall. I pull the trigger one last time as his fist hits my wounded side while driving me through canvas curtains that protect a work area. I drop into inky darkness..

I must be dead. Strangely there is pain and a great weight on my chest. I am breathing. That's interesting. I slowly come up out into the light. The Womp's face is next to mine. Empty, fish dead, eyes stare intensely at the floor. Hay! Hay! The Womp is dead, the wicked Womp is dead. Sorry I am not all there.

I shove the corpse from me. It takes what little strength I have, to shift his bulk. Finally, I lay quietly having at least passed that hurdle. The ceiling of the structure hangs above like a grayish sky.I should be exhilarated by the fact that I am alive but I am not.

Perhaps in a perfect world men kill other men and walk away without regret or fear. I cannot. I realize that I am doomed like a man with cancer. My soul is damned. I know in my inner self that my face must have mirrored the murderer's evil glare. I know that I have taken life without reason, for there is no reason to deprive others of life. I have survived but feel nothing. Better them then me. Yes! there is that. I have a family to return to, tied to me by love. I have tried to protect them by my actions but realize that the evil is too great. The Womp is dead but nineteen more stand in the hazy distance killing others even now. What have I accomplished? The right, yes, also I have given others the privilege of breathing another day. That too is something. Perhaps it is that someone must sacrifice. That their small chip must be placed against the darkness because others cannot defend themselves. The average police officer would call me a fool. So be it. I cannot undo what I have done and would not. I will carry the load. There is no glory just survival.

The concrete was cold. I tried to sit up and realize that my body is covered with blood. My clothing is saturated and a large pool surrounds me. The thirty two caliber shell in my cane gun has torn through the Womp's pumping heart. My God how long have I been here? I make a mental note to remove the Special Services Section from my Christmas list. I rise to my feet using my trusty cane to lever myself off the floor.

Before opening the curtain I pause and reach down to remove the Womp's ring and chain. The two rings are basically the same, one slightly more intricate. Maybe that is an indication of a higher personage on the food chain. I didn't care.

I pushed the curtain aside. Only one plane faced me.

Chapter Thirteen - Laguardia Airport, New York, New York, USA

High Flight Inc.

For a moment I held on to the heavy canvas that surrounded the work area and the Ring Womp's body. I needed the support. One plane was gone, removed when I was out cold. The Womp would know which plane. It would have to be this one. He had waited to make sure it left. That is why he was still in the hangar when I arrived.

My mind now spins. Three hundred people are in peril what am I going to do? An excellent question. In an ER the surgeons should be taking time to make the best and most prudent decision for the patient. In many cases there is no time, hesitation kills the patient, faster and more certainly then action .

I must act. The authorities, airport police, gallop to mind. A telephone tip would not work. My running into a cop covered with blood screaming that a plane was about to be destroyed would place me a) In the loony bin, b) In the local clink until everyone checked out everything. I can tell you from experience things in the police services never move as quickly as on the television. By the time,

everybody had called everybody, the plane would be
in Germany. More realistically it would be under
about six hundred feet of water. c) I could be held
for the murder of the Womp, who it must be
remembered had no record and really shouldn't
have been in the hangar but that wasn't a killing
offence. I could of course tell them he had shot me
first but they would date the wound and that would
have proved me a liar. Over and above that my
identification would require questions. I had been
given a synopsis of my interior designer altar ego. . I
tried to memorize the created history but in a pinch I
couldn't hope to answer any kind of solid questions.
I could call Dell at CIA or the embassy and have
them intercede. Both of those concepts would take
time.

Think! What do I do? I get on the plane. I then
convince the pilot I am telling the truth . I had
visions of that little conversation, especially if the
Deutscher in question couldn't understand English.
He also might think I was just some poor nut. I
didn't have the time for that. The plane might have
already flown, if so I had to know right away. If the
plane was in the air then the question became a non
sequitur.

First I would need clothing. My pants had only a
small amount of blood on them. The jacket and

shirt had to go. I look around and find the Womp's
bag sitting on the floor. Inside are a change of
clothing and his leather jacket. I strip to the waist
and then move over to the sink by the wall. With
some gritty soap used to remove oil and grease. I
scrub off the blood and watch it flow away. The
bandage is soaked through but Marg had placed a
plastic contact sheet over the wound to hold my
blood in. At least I didn't have to worry about
AIDS right now. At least I hoped not.

I put the polo shirt over my head with slow
agonizing movements and almost pass out again.

The sections of the broken rib are rubbing against
each other. The pain is intense. A towel is provided
for drying your hands. It's one of those that loop
back into the machine as it is pulled down for use .
Once the towel is completely pulled through it is
changed. I remove the pocket knife which is small
but very sharp and removed the towel. By wrapping
it around my middle as tightly as possible and then
tying off ends made by cutting into the material
everything seems to be more in place. It still hurts
like hell. Finally I put his leather jacket over
everything else and move out.

Outside I see a small Luftliepzig baggage train
headed for the main debarkation area. I flag the

driver down and ask if he will give me a lift cause I'm leaving for Germany on the plane that they just took over to the loader shoot. Duffy, the driver, says sure in a Bronx accent , I have the Womp's I'dent dog tag around my neck with my picture quickly cut out and inserted for his.

" That's her right over ther." Duffy points and I jump on. The ride is quick and pleasant as Duffy asks about my trip. I tell him I had an accident falling down a flight of stairs and now that I was over the physio, it was off to Munich for two weeks.

Duffy who has been there, tells me I should see various sights. I try to look like I am listening. But to be honest it is all a dream . I am passing out again. I whack my rib with my elbow. That wakes me up alright. Duffy asks if I'm all right cause I look kind of white.

I say I'll be alright when I get enough beer in me. He laughs and leaves me at the base of the loading area. I enter the door nearest me and get lost. I finally have to ask a girl in the office where the debarkation area is because I'm new. She looks kind of questioning but tells me as if it were against her better judgement.

I run to the Luftliepzig ticket counter. Well, I hobble at my best pace. The flight 897 Berlin is being called for embarkation. I stop and wait behind seven other people, for what seems an interminable period. Finally, I am before the girl and ask for a ticket providing a Gold Card.. I am late but I can make it if I run. She sees my cane and I smile sadly. In a moment, I am being run over to embarkation on a golf cart put aside for just this purpose. With German precision, I am dropped just as Flight 897 is closing. The employee with me in the cart asks the girl to wait. She looks a little perturbed until she sees me hobble toward her. She immediately calls to the plane to hold on. I pass through, all I have is the Womp's clothing and my cane. In a moment my British Passport is checked and I am let by.

I enter the plane and hear the door close behind me. I am placed in remembrance of the coffin cover making the same firm noise. I must now get to the other end of the airbus to see the Captain. The plane is gigantic and seems interminable. I have a first class ticket and am not stopped. The engines start.

I hesitate for a moment leaning on a seat to catch my breath and allow the pain to subside. Instantly, I seem to be in a tornado, then blackness.

I feel the plane as it suffers some turbulence. This wakes me up disoriented and belted into a seat. I figure it must have been empty and available when I collapsed into it. The stu had belted me in with standard German efficiency. How long? God! How

long? We were in the air. I look at my Epsylon and
realize we have been up for over fifteen minutes. I
move toward the front of the plane once more.

I am confronted by an attractive blond stu who
asks where my seat is, as I look befuddled. I look
her in the eye as intently as possible and ask to
speak to the pilot.

"That is impossible. The pilot is involved with
flying the plane. Perhaps I can ask one of the air
crew to speak with you later."

"Listen closely,' I say as clearly and calmly as
possible. 'I saw a known Swiss terrorist come out of
the hangar this plane was in. I am uncertain if he
damaged the plane but I purchased a ticket to tell
the pilot . Unfortunately I passed out, I have had an
accident and I am still not very steady. If I am right
we have about fifteen minutes to get back to the
airport." Her face shows fear and uncertainty

"I am sure you were mistaken. Perhaps it was
someone else." She tries to calm me.

"No, I am a part time policeman in England. I am
sure. I must talk to the pilot." The definition, tone
and the absolute certainty on my part make her
unsure.

I know there is security on the plane. I am about to

see it. She says she will be right back. I move closer
to the front of the plane. I see her speak quickly and
confidently into the telephone. There is a phone call
for a Mr. Lunger. Please come to the number three
booth. This in German floats over the plane sound
system. Lunger is about what I expect. He moves
quickly as possible to the sight . He is large and a
little over weight but he will do the job if required.
He stops and talks to the stu. She points to me as
she describes the situation. I move forward. Lunger
turns to face me.

"You are a policeman, Nie?" he demands but in a
soft smooth voice.

"Reserve Policeman," I correct him. He nods. In
his mind I am going nowhere near the pilot or the
control area yet.

"Describe what you saw." he asks again not
unkindly.

"The man is Jean Monblanc, or at least that is his
name of choice. I saw a sheet on him."

"You are not British, Nie?" The German was
quick.

"No originally I am Canadian but I lived in Britain
for some time."

"So! You are here because?" All of this was quite proper but the time was passing.

"Listen , I don't know what he did to the plane but if it works like the others, we have about 12 minutes to turn around and get down. I show him my watch.
" I need to talk to the pilot now." I keep my voice down but I am emphatic.

The questions for Lunger are, am I some nut? Is this the ranting of a mad man? What will I do if he doesn't play along? The decision is his and not his.

"A moment while I call ,Nie?" He picks up the phone I move up to where he is and listen.

"Let us go to the front of the plane. He says softly. We move as quickly as I can. Finally, we are just behind the cockpit in a metal safe room. It is small but will take a lot of damage. Lunger. Frisks me and finds nothing but the fact that I am held together with tape. I ask to sit and he nods.

He asks the captain to come out. Captain Pilot Albert Otto Helsnen is the son of a pig farmer who now flies the largest planes in the Luftliepzig fleet. He is very competent and very well versed in the ways of the world. He enters the room and closes the connection with the cockpit firmly behind him. His is six foot tall. Has an open honest face with ocean blue eyes, a roman nose and large lips. I look at my watch.

"There is no terrorist named Monblanc and you are listed as an interior decorator." He says this in very precise English. There is no place for error here. He will not take any crap.

" I killed this man Monblanc in the hangar back at Laguardia."

"He tried to kill me. His body is behind the curtain around the work area. He had half an hour in the hangar before I could get to him. What he did to this plane in that time I have no idea. It might be too late already but if we look at the other times this happened, we have about ten minutes to get back to the airport." He looked incredulous.

" I am to believe this? Are you mad?"

"You have three hundred people on this plane. If I'm wrong then they get inconvenienced and you can toss me in the deepest cell they have in New York. If not though, we all die." My clear definition of the situation really gets to him. He has a slight tic at the side of his mouth. At the moment he is uncertain.

"You say you killed a man."

"Yes," He looks at me coldly.

"He did you no harm.

"We grappled he broke my rib. I shot him."

"Are you armed?" He looks at Lunger and stiffens

"No." the security man says.

" I left the gun behind. I never could have gotten on the plane. One of his confederates shot me last night." Otto looks at Lunger again.

"He is taped up. There is a lot of blood." Lunger looks scared now.

"I risked my life to save you and the people on your plane. It may be too late but we have to try to get back." He cuts me off.

"Get the doctor, he is in seat 91. Now! Schnell."

"Ja herr Captain. Lunger snaps too. Otto almost has his mind made up.

"You're wasting time." I accuse

"We will see.' He snarled. 'you are not a British policeman."

"I am a kind of British Policeman. I meet his eyes."

"Spion, a spy." he accuses and looks like he might spit in my eye.

The doctor is a small man on his way back to his children in Bremen, after a enjoyable but costly tour of the United States. He is upset at being called into action. I figure he should ask who will pay him in a moment. Otto has no time for that kind of garbage.

"Check this man see if he has been shot. It is of the utmost importance to all of us."

The man has kind hands. He helps me to remove my shirt. The dirty towel and crimson bandage are revealed. He unwraps my middle as easily as possible. A moment later he confirms the rib. The second bandage comes off more quickly. The wound looks like minced meat from where I sit.

"Mien Gott! " Lungér chimes in.

"This man should be in a hospital." The Herr doctor says.

"I apologize." says Otto and disappears into the cockpit. The plane starts to turn slowly but perceptibly.

I hear Otto's hard flat voice above and around me.

"We are returning to Laguardia there are minor technical problems but we do not wish to take any chances. Please remain calm there is no reason for concern."

"The doctor shoots me full of pain killer, then antibiotics, a local anaesthetic follows. He then re stitches the areas of the wound, the Womp has broken. I get a new bandage which feels more comfortable. Finally a rewrap of my ribs this time properly. I feel considerably better.

"You must lie down" He says in his kind voice. The forty something face etched with wrinkles centered by sensitive blue eyes, a large nose and tight straight mouth smiles at me, to give encouragement.

"I think I'll sit doc, but thanks for everything. I'll be all right now."

"You have a strong constitution, yes? That is the word, Ja?"

"Yes, you're absolutely right. Too stupid to die." We both smile. I look at my watch we should both be dead. I feel the plane drop in a slow glide. Old Otto isn't taking any chances. If something goes pop he wants to be low enough to allow for decompression.

I sit quietly then ask Lunger to get me a drink.

"Whiskey." I ask looking at the doctor.

"Good, I will join you.' The tired face says. 'How much time do you think we might have?" He asks directly. I forget he has probably been asked the same question many times. I wonder how he delivered the answer?

" Like the Herr Captain says, only minor technical difficulties. I really don't know." I finish more honestly.

"I will go and hold hands with my wife. We have been married for twenty-five years and I still am in love with her. I think I would like to be with her now. If you will permit me?"

"Sure doc. I envy you and thank you.' We shake hands and he moves off.

Lunger returns with two whiskey's. He is on duty. I suggest he join me but he won't." The first one goes down straight. I feel the burning right to my stomach. The second I sip.

I sit thinking someone should sing "Closer My God To Thee."

I settle in the seat without a window and sip my whiskey making ready for the roar or the rending of metal or the rush of wind . I know the time to death will be less than seconds. Our chances in the front of the plane were less 50-50 at best. However, it depended how we went in. I calculate the many ways we can die. Then the words of High Flight come to me.

" Reached out my hand and touched the face of

God." The poem is written by a pilot about flying and seems to fit the moment.

There is a lot more but I can't remember. I will try to reach out my hand and touch God's face but I fear all I will touch is air until my heart stops, the last kindness of the human body, before we hit.'

The plane picks up speed. Every ripple in the movement of the plane tears through my body. Each breath is the last one. I look at Lunger who is scared as I am. I decide to think of someone else.

" You own a dog Lunger?"

"What?' The security man is taken aback. 'A dog Yes. I have a a dog."

"What kind?"

"What ?Oh! It is a great furry thing. It will come to the name Hiedi. My little girl named it. She is only five." I hear his voice crack.

" My dog is an old flee bag. Lots of hair too. You never know which end you're talking to." I smile. Lunger smiles too.

I hear the roar and grab the chair until my knuckles whiten.

Chapter fourteen - 7:20 P.m. The Luftlietzig
Hangar, Laguardia Airport, New York.

The Razors End

I believed the sweetest sound I have ever heard,
was the soft language of the Caribbean in song. I
was wrong. It was the kiss of rubber on a wet
tarmac. Old Otto brought the big plane into the
debarkation tube like the pro he was. Based on my
suggestion, the problem probably wouldn't be a
bomb. Otto didn't deploy the foam chutes and have
people slide out.

At the moment three hundred odd passengers were
making calls to waiting relatives and grumbling
about the service, a short ways away in a protected
visitors' lounge.

I sat in a metal chair while two sets of Luftleipzig
mechanics went over the plane. The search was
carried on with precision and accuracy as only such
matters can be handled in the German community.

Flanking me were two local police officers along
with representatives of the airport force. A few
moments after that two FBI people showed up. The
conversation over jurisdiction was muted, given the
situation with the plane but you knew it was already
underway.

The Womp was gone. He had disappeared along with his great pool of blood, my saturated jacket shirt and any other modicum that would define his being or end.. All the locals had was my word for the fact he existed. His bag with a passport and some other small items lent credence to my story.

No body, no charges but of course there was the little matter of stopping a Trans-Atlantic airliner in mid flight because a nonexistent terrorist had fiddled with it.

Otto watched with cold anger. His sideways glances at me were not pleasant.

I of course was surrounded in the impenetrable armor of the knowledge that I had told the truth and done my best. Right!

I ask the FBI types to call Langley and contact Dell. I give my name and his extension.
The flip phone is in action immediately.

Dell is available. The two American security types pass on information. Finally, admitting that I was about six foot, a little overweight and yes, ugly as sin.

At that point I politely asked them to tell Dell that he could f.. himself and the horse he road in on. That brought a lot of laughter and an invitation to tell him myself. I am passed the phone.

"I hear your non-killing people again." Dell starts in.

"Yeah! You ought to hire these guys. They do a better clean up job then your goons."

"No one is that good." Dell holds up the CIA's end. Then I get real tense.

"Listen up these guy's are part of some kind of European secret society. The Avengers of the Ring."
" They all got Uncle Wiggley decoder bands or what?" Dell was making fun but I knew he was listening. I could picture his big solid Midwestern face tensing up to hear the worst.

"These boys have been killing people since the crusades if you can believe that? They're very wealthy and cover themselves real well. This Ring man was in with the plane for half an hour before I could trace him. I was using one of those Chinese heat signature units."

"Those things are knockoffs of the Russian product and it was crap." Dell gives his opinion

"Yeah I know but it worked this time. Unfortunately my problem is I'm a little shot up."

"How bad.' Give it what you will Dell almost seemed to care. I smiled to myself.

"I'm fine. I think they're going to find whatever it is he left. If not I'd like to walk. One, I killed this guy fair and square. He instigated it and I finished it. He's been disappeared so no charges. Two, the plane is OK and I only tried to help. I'm not taking the rap for that. Fix it will you. I figure Uncle Sam owes me one for Thunderbay.

"OK, I'll see what I can do."

"Dell listen there was no one in this hangar for more than a hour. That's a hell of a long time."

"I'll check it out Mike "

"Dell just knowing about these birds could get you killed, so watch who you tell."

"Nice of you tell me now. I saw the fax from London. A lot of people know"

Dell rings off. I never was Dell's favorite person but we at least got along. The blue brotherhood held certain sway even here. I figured he would take care of it for me?

I will not attempt to address the sheer nerve-racking terror of flying in your own coffin. In knowing that others were out there, good honest people who just happened to take the wrong flight. A decision that placed themselves in this disaster looking for a place to happen. Fortunately only the Doctor had a real grasp of the problem. The rest might be a little frightened. However, the plane coasted in with the minimum trouble and maximum safety.

I, on the other hand, count each second. The mind takes over and you think what can happen. What will I do? Well, to be honest I die, unless the scenario is uniquely good for me.

The men scramble about the major mechanical components, lifting engines out, removing and checking areas. Sniffer dogs do a run through. The chemical boys are also asked in. They of course will go first followed by the bomb squad. Every piece of luggage is double checked. Each compartment given a complete going over. The frustration is mounting and I have a pretty good concept of who the end receiver of all this dissatisfaction will be.

I sit quietly, with my face in my hands and hear the rattle. Not glass, mind you, small fragments of plastic or metal sliding down the outside skin of the airplane. I look up and watch more of the chips fall. As the workman who has caused the shower moves to a second window over the wing and taps the top of the frame with the same result.

"Mein Got en Himmel." He cries out then a compete evaluation of the situation in German. I already know the secret and it's beautiful, terribly, primitively, perfect. The Womp had removed the interior insulation from the window top and replaced it with a standard caulking. The plane would reach thirty-five thousand feet and the 100 degree below zero cold up there would turn the caulking into brittle paint. The first strain the

slightest violent shift and the fascia would fall out
or fracture. That would in turn allow the killer cold
to enter the body of the airbus.

The cold would come as a stealthy assassin,
quickly putting the passengers to sleep. In fifteen
seconds their bodies would be lifeless. The air
system would penetrate the cockpit. At that point
the plane was doomed unless the air masks fell and
the half sane Otto could drop the aircraft fifteen
thousand feet in say five seconds. Then pull out and
not terminally damage the fuselage. The
possibilities were slim to none. The crime was a
done deal. A simple accident how could they define
otherwise from the shreds of metal and other debris
that the American coast guard finally dragged up.

Lonely pained survivors of the dead would cling to
the pain, as that was all there was. Standing on
some ship or by some sand spit crying their last
farewell. All that pain, all that agony, for what? The
death of one or two people who counted? The rest
were simply bystanders, back ground, no more than
trash .

Otto looked around to apologize and try to explain
what had happened but my chair was empty.

While the two FBI guys made a half hearted
search, I was already at the Hertz counter swiping

my gold card and making my getaway in a new
Lincoln Town Car. Special Services , accounting
and Granny, for that matter could go to blazes. I got
out onto the I-95 and headed south.

It was good to be in charge of my life once more. It
was wonderful to control where I went and how I
got there. I would never take a plane again, sure!
There was no tail. I motored along enjoying the soft
Virginia country side. I reached Richmond,
bypassed the city, took the second cut off and went
to the Holiday Inn which sat nearby. I pulled into a
local mall. I purchased a cheep carry bag, some
small toiletries a change of clothing, including a
new lightweight jacket and some pajamas.
Fortunately the major shops are still open. I
purchase a Toshiba Lap Top as the lights when out.

I then signed in at the hotel, entered the soft green
room that offered television and net hookup. I
secured the door, removed my clothing and lay on
the bed. I found it a little cold in the air-
conditioning. I sat up on the bed covered my legs
and tapped out a full report to Epsylon, in code,
through Brit Line.

Granny was not overjoyed. I had blown my cover,
not followed procedures, left Marg in the lurch and
finally broken every rule in the book. At the end,

after venting his spleen, there was this short message. 'Oh, By the way congratulations on saving aircraft. Go Home that is a direct order.'

" I start to type once more. I informed my fearless leader I would be on St. Martin tomorrow. At that point I would clear up all the loose ends. I will contact him at that time. I log off and shut the machine down. I then change hotels.

Sleep is such a sweet thing, it refreshes the human body. Sleep regenerates, it sweeps away the problems of the day before. I woke up refreshed at six in the morning. I did more of a wash than a shower because of my bandages but this was, at least, refreshing. I order a couple of eggs sunny side up, some bacon and toast. This is washed down with a large glass of fresh orange juice.

I sit back and peruse the local Richmond paper. The publication seems to have limited information concerning the plane problem at Laguardia. However, there seemed to be a move in Congress for more clearly defined checks on planes with over a certain number of hours service. As some small cracks had been found in various places, including window fittings. The Womps are warned as are all other aircraft owners . It would be interesting to see who buys it for this little disaster on the Womp side but we will never know.

I sit back and make notes as to what has to be done. I will make contact with Peter Zealander of Her Majesty's Netherlands Secret Service. Peter and I went way back and I figured he would help out. I would also have to call Superintendent Maurice St Armand of the French police on Guadeloupe. Most importantly I had to stop in and see Harry. He was not dead but close . Come hell or high water I would see Harry. He meant more to me then the rest of this stupid thing put together..

Then I was going to kill someone. Not because he threatened me. It simply it had to be done because he had killed and would continue to kill. It had to be done before he killed me or someone else on our side.

I would become what I had promised myself I never would be, a man who would destroy life without provocation, who no longer stayed within the bounds of the law and its fragile limits. I would become my own law just this once. Could there be only once.? Was there another name for murder?

I was on the road by six-thirty the next morning. I was refreshed but hurting in many places. I guessed my wound was somewhat better. I would look into it on St Martin . I drive down the 95 until I can cut over to the I 79 and take a plane from Columbia, South Carolina to Miami, where I change for the

Caribbean.

Juliana airport on St Martin had not changed.
Perhaps it was more crowded in the early afternoon.
I go through customs, it is a slow process as I have
used the last of the pain pills provided by the Herr
Doctor, as a parting gift .Every movement now hurt.

Outside in the seventy degree heat, Peter stands by
an ice, green Honda Civic. I am pleased to see him.

I am here after a short stop in Road Town on
Tortola in the British Virgin islands. In a clean but
small private room lay Harry with tubes coming out
of his nose and other parts of his body. Phil sits in a
corner of the room and smiles as I enter. I nod in
return.

Harry tries to smile but it is wan he is very white
but will survive, so the doctor tells me. The
operation was one of the longest in the hospitals
history and the Governor had taken direct interest. I
say a small prayer to thank God for Harry's
survival. It makes me feel better just knowing he
will return to his cottage and be there when I call.
We all need a little constancy in our lives; in a spy's
life that is even more important.

"Dogging it again?" I accuse. Harry woofs a little
but it hurts. I sit and I drop a three comic books
next to the wounded spy.

"Christ on a crutch! Just what I wanted, funny papers.' He eyes me jaundicely. I laugh out loud as does Phil behind me. 'I was just lying here clinging to life " Harry continues, 'hoping some git would traipse in here and bring the latest copy of the Broom Family." The sarcasm is tangible.

" When I was a kid and I was sick my dad always brought me a comic book to cheer me up.' I explain. 'So when I visit someone in Hospital or where ever they're goofing off I bring them a comic. That was all they had at the airport." I finish with a wan smile feeling a little foolish. However, I know good old Harry will survive. Sarcasm is an undeniable indicator.

"Under those circumstances, thank you. I feel exceedingly more cheery then five minutes ago." He coughs. And I stiffen but it passes.

"I think I can understand the talk I heard about having your liver bronzed for being such a scout about everything."

"They can bloody well try." says the unrepentant Harry.

"How are you?" I ask to be polite

"Oh! Jolly wonderful,' he continues in the same vain, ' I and Phil will be off for a ripping game of tennis in a half a mo. You're lucky I could fit you in on my cluttered schedule."

"Look I'd love to exchange insults but I was told

I've got very little time. Also I have things to do.' I stop for a moment then get right to it. 'How did this happen?"

"I was having a talk with your friend the Toad . The Bastard just walked in and shot me in the back.. I didn't see him. I thought it was the warder bringing in tea and I wasn't taking my eyes off that fat ,bald terp."

"Pimple say anything.?"

"No he seemed to be a closed mouth type with the exception of fowl language for which he had a real gift. The ticket for the ship was purchased with cash"

" I figure Bessy got it from the same source."

"Don't think so the timing was off. I think the Chinese flew someone in from Panama to do the job. Paying debts, old boy." Harry was getting tired.

" Fine, look Harry get well. I owe you a bottle, we'll share it."

"Granny is mad as a hatter" Harry says concerned. 'What the hell happened?"

"I'm going to balance the budget Harry. A lot of bills need paying. You, the warder, Jerry, Megel and seven good men, thirty years ago."

"If you have to, do it cold, not hot." Harry warned.

"I'll try. First I have to be sure."

Chapter fifteen - 9:30 A.m. Simpson Beach, St.
Maarten, Dutch West Indies.

The Search.

Simpson Beach borders the airport. Given my
last couple of days experience with flight, I suppose,
I might have found a different more quiet spot for
reflection. I am under doctor's orders not to over do
anything. As the Netherlands is aiding me with my
investigation and paying for all this luxury, I am
being good.

The soft waves lethargically spread out up the
sandy beach. Then as if fatigued by so much work
slide back slowly into their own vastness. Along
the tide line small children play in the sand
watched by mothers in various swim suit designs. I
enjoy the scene. I am still coming down and need
as many restful moments as possible.

I while away the time on the beach, as things are
moving forward in my master plan. Well, I am just
looking into what I know but at least it's movement.
At present, I am in poor shape to do much more
right now.

I eat breakfast under a large umbrella in a
comfortable chair. A bacon omelet provides lots of
protein. Toast, thickly spread with butter piled with

strawberry jam, black coffee that smells of the Indies and a fruit plate. Apples, oranges, pears, kiwi and other brightly coloured morsels are spread out on a platter ready to mouth down, in comfortable bites.

I am the guest of the Dutch Governor whose personal physician has laid on all of this splendor. Holland has always liked Canadians. We freed them from the nazis during World War Two and they have a long memory. Each year Ottawa, the Canadian Capital, explodes with multi coloured tulips, a gift from that thankful nation.

In my case, I performed work on the island which saved a number of young women in peril. This made the local police and military look very good which is not forgotten either. The result of that good deed is that at this very moment, Peter Zealander is searching his computer, with the consent of The Hague, for cross references to Russian agents that the four murdered Dutch operatives might have been involved with. Their deaths as well as two of our own agents and a French spy were linked together as the work of one Jewel Dubois back in 1962. Dubois had been the senior British operative in the Caribbean. This at the time of the Bay of Pigs invasion of Cuba, by the CIA. The slain men were key players in the intelligence system down here and their removal more or less destroyed our

source system. This was just prior to the American
blockade which almost brought the world to nuclear
war. At that time the deaths were considered
payback for the invasion and the assistance the
various colonial governments had provided.. This
was done on the part of the Cubans and their
Russian allies. Dubois had escaped to New Orleans
where he had connections and survived until last
year when he paid 'big time,' for his sins.

   Dubois deserved to die perhaps more for other
reasons but it did give a satisfactory finality to a
long open case file. The question at hand was, "Was
that really the end?" I will find out soon.

   I feel immensely better. Doctor Van Fluten a
young pleasant faced man, who was balding,
although he was no more than thirty, had made sure
I stayed in the hospital. Peter took me in late
yesterday after I almost passed out getting into the
car. A large sedative effectively knocked me out
after his examination. This morning grudgingly, I
had been let loose. Only over the doctors protest and
because Peter and the Governor seemed to agree it
would be best. I am told to do nothing but watch the
sea and rest. At the moment I am pleased to do just
that. My wound is getting better. This in spite of
my careless attempts to make it worse.

My wife is worried. I have made contact with her through the Cleveland cut off. My twenty year old is out all night and she as all mothers is upset. I remind her we spent nights out and her parents had a cow. She is not placated. The rest of my mob are well and number one son is no worse for wear.

She asks as to my health and I lie of course. I will be home in two days or less. I also mention that I love her and want her. She indicates she might be willing. I hope to hell I am better by then but I have my doubts.

The wind blows in fresh and sweet. I am reminded of Jerry and Megel who will never enjoy it again. This brings to mind my last sight of Harry Breakleaf who will be in bed for a month or more. My face must have reflected my inner anger. Peter's smile disappeared as he slipped into my rest area stealing a piece of fruit from the platter as he sat. "Something wrong?" He asks. Yes everything but nothing that should disturb you. I say inwardly.

"No! How did you make out? " I ask off handedly.

"Not bad for thirty years ago." He says wolfing down another piece of kiwi, then wiping his fingers on my napkin.

"Can I know?" I ask politely.

"Sure." He smiles. 'only two of them, Van Key and Sangter, had interaction with same agents, from the

other side. There are four of them.' He placed two
blurry pictures of Soviet agents on the table . 'We
only have photo's of these, the others aren't in the
files or have been lost." I look at the pictures but
they are not who I am expecting.

"No! It's not them." I shake my head.

"He places four report faxes on the table . I look at
the information as it is translated into English and
remove the ones we know aren't tied to this matter.
The other two are the right age but one Kenirinof is
dead . He died in Austria ten years ago. This is
marked on the sheet. That leaves the other.
Alexander Demetri Youdonavich. The information
is limited. He worked in the Netherlands for a short
time prior to the Bay of Pigs. Interestingly enough
he also worked in Belgium. There was a side report
on his activities from a Belgian Security Officer.

"It says here he was in Belgium, I wonder if they
would have a picture?" I ask

"Everything is possible but it would take weeks.
They're worse than the French sometimes." Says
Peter eating more of my fruit tray.

"Tell them you're Leopard's cousin." I suggest
smiling with reptilian bonhomery.

"Sure any thing for you.' agrees Peter, ' Just a
minute and I'll grow another head. How important
is this?"

"I need to know by tonight." I say without a question in my voice.

"So, you shall have it." Peter confirms grabbing more cut orange as he makes off.

I take out my trusty cell phone which has followed me to the British Virgins, courtesy of the Phil and good old Dell who covers for me as he said he would. The package includes my pachyderm which is also loaded. It is fitting I think that I have Jerry's gun for this last part of my mission That is if it materializes. At this point I don't have much more then a hunch.

My phone call to the French Colony of Guadeloupe is made through France and is almost instantaneously connected. The Gendarme who answers listens to my Quebecois French and tells me that Chief Inspector St Armand is in but at this point indisposed. I ask him to mention my name. Maurice is on the phone in two minutes. This reaction is not because of any love lost. The Chief Inspector is not one of my biggest fans.

"Console my Ulcer and tell me you are not on French soil." He starts off. I can see his lean Gaelic face with the intense brown eyes and his silver sweep of hair above a furrowed brow, in my mind's eye.. If things are as usual his blue kepi is resting on the desk at his right as always.

"In absolute honesty, I can say without contradiction, that I am not on the hallowed soil of the Republic." I say laughing.

"Bon! What is it you want.? I hope this has nothing to do with kidnapped French Nationals." Maurice doesn't hesitate. We move right to the chase.

"No! In 1962, February, a man was shot in Guadeloupe. He was taken to the local hospital where he survived his wound. I want to know where he was shot." I say.

"In Guadeloupe one would suspect." Said the Chief Inspector. The sarcasm was not lost on me.

"I mean in what area of his body was he shot." I correct myself.

"Do I get the name of this worthy individual?" Maurice demands figuring rightly that there is more to this deal then meets the eye.

I give the cover name of the man I am following up on.

"Bien, I will see what we have." He brings the conversation to an end.

"I need the information by six tonight. Lives depend on it Maurice." I grow intense and St. Armand hesitates.

"French lives?" He demands.

"Yes." I say honestly. At this point I am unsure

what will happen.

"Bien! You will have it." Maurice gives his word
there is nothing more sure once that commitment is
made.

"Thank you, Maurice." I say honestly.

"It is my duty to defend the lives of French
citizens anywhere in the world." And with that he
hung up. I was chastened but pleased.

The end of the day was nie. In paradise this comes
with a slow mindless quiet. Soon the air will be
filled with music and night life. The people of St.
Marrtin will start to jump or party . However , for
the moment there is peace. The small traffic jam at
five is over. Philipsberg's lights twinkle into the
dusk. Europeans tend to eat later then we in North
America. They also take the time, like the Japanese,
to enjoy the meal, unlike us.

I have not eaten and will not, until much later, if
at all. I am dressed in light cotton khaki pants and a
white open necked shirt. My Panama Jack is pulled
down low. I am ready . I have made the fateful
telephone call and await dusk to make my
rendezvous with a man I will kill.

Maurice had called back and gives me his
information. As soon as, the Chief Inspector

identified where the man had been shot, all those years ago, I was sure. If that had not been the case, Peter wandered into the hotel bar only a half an hour ago, to hand me a picture the Belgians had provided. What it cost to the Netherlands Government in good will, I had no idea but it must be have been astronomical . Now there was no mistake but the taste in my mouth was sour. I wished I had been wrong. I wished I had never become a spy. However, I had taken the Ladie's tin and must provide my services at Her command. I had given my word and would always fulfill it while I lived.

Chapter sixteen - 8:05 P.m. La Rue St. Louie,
Marigot, St. Martin, French West Indies.

To Tell The Truth

The Rue St Louis is at the far North of the town of
Marigot the capital of French, St. Martin. The island
is shared by the two colonial empires. The Dutch to
the south in Philipsburg. France here in this little
bit of the Mediterranean coast transplanted into the
West Indies.

Marigot has a magical substance in the dusk, as
the heat slowly declines. The soft colours of the half
night turn the city into a set of paintings by Degas
and Monet. Grays and purples, soft pinks,
mystically leave an elegant town with a romantic
dream like quality. I have been here many times as a
courier. At those times I had enjoyed the soft
colours, had had my senses and my spirit lifted by
the picturesque beauty of the Rue St. Louie with its
selection of white walled bungalows.

I would arrive early just to walk down this small
street and soak up that moment at dusk just before
dinner with Henry Say.

Of course, I had no inkling then of the danger this
had placed me in. Henry had saved my life when I
had escaped Vincent Au Clair. In doing so, I saved

Yatomi the Japanese school girl, his organization
had kidnapped from a Tokyo street . Removing her
from the clutches of this truly evil man had made us
fugitives. Au Clair had members of the local police
in his pocket. Henry had allowed us to hide in his
home and helped us if grudgingly to overcome the
villain.

I sat on a small bench across the street from his
home and waited for 8:15 and our prescribed
meeting time. The quiet magic of the street had a
strange affect on me. It made me unsure of what I
was doing. Was this right ? I had broken bread with
this man. He had placed himself at personal risk to
save me or had he. Should I confront him without a
gun and allow him to answer the charges I had
developed or simply kill him. Could I simply kill?

I am many things. Some of these things I am not
proud of. Six people had died because of my actions
in the last three days. All of these individuals had
threatened my existence or that of someone I loved.
I had taken the action prescribed. It was less
difficult all the time to question the acts. In the end,
I believed these actions were morally right. To kill
Henry without trial was murder. What if I was
wrong? I learned at a very young age I was not God.
However, I knew in myself, I wasn't wrong and that
was the rub.

I sat in the late evening shade playing with the wide brim of my Panama Jack. The question that perhaps bothered me most came to mind. Could I look my kids in the eye and tell them truthfully their father was a killer? Not a simple soldier doing his duty in a shadow war but a cold blooded murderer without remorse.

I had made a long report in code and shipped it in. Based on that, Granny would look into the matter. However, while this was personal, the knowledge Say possessed could cripple our Secret Service and others. That could not happen. If I confronted him, he would be warned. It would also give him the chance to kill me first. He could disappear, escape justice and do damage elsewhere. My choice was clear. I sat and watched the colours change, steeling myself for what I must do.

I heard the footsteps or sensed them. They came toward me at a measured but comfortable pace. I figured one of the locals out for a short walk. I glanced to my right and looked into the china blue eyes of Theodore (Granny) Boothby-Staters, Head of the North American Department of Her Majesty's Secret Service and my immediate superior. I do not think I have ever been so glad to see anyone in my entire life.

"Hi Boss take a pew " I smile and indicate the

bench. If I had been a little more sensitive to the situation, I would have noticed Granny's cold indifferent stare. However, my offer made him smile too and shake his head.

"No I'll stand. " He says leaning against the nearest tree.

"Beautiful isn't it?" I ask

"Yes very." He confirms.

" I came here tonight to kill Henry Say. Well, not Henry Say. He died back in 1962 or early '63. I came to kill Alexander Demetri Youdonavich, KGB and Russian Intelligence agent . He killed Jerry and it was my mistake that caused it." I fished in my shirt pocket for the grainy black and white picture, Peter had provided. This I handed to Granny who stiffed visibly and tensed as if I were going to do him some harm. I noticed this in passing but then he didn't get out in the field much anymore and maybe that was the reason.

'Scary isn't it?" I asked as he looked at the blurred picture. " They probably didn't have to make too many changes to make the switch. Mainly around the eyes, I would think."

It was a troika of course and we bought it hook line and sinker."

" You say you caused Jerry's death?' Granny said softly

"Yes, I missed a little thing. Just a small insignificant thing. The devil is always in the details. I saw Henry without his shirt. That was why I had to die. It was why he got Pimple to throw me overboard. When I didn't have the good grace to die as expected, he had to figure we were on to him. We were watching Pimple as you know. Say must have realized we didn't know who was behind that gormless buffoon and got rid of Jerry and Megel figuring we would think it was Toad who did the shooting.."

" What was significant about seeing Henry without his shirt?" Asked Granny probably trying to fathom the story as it came out of me.

"Our Henry Say went out to the Caribbean and was stationed on Anguilla in 62. He was sent to Guadeloupe. I don't know why but they tried to kill him there . I checked in with Maurice St. Armand today. They shot our Henry in the abdomen. The bullet went right through. This Henry Say hasn't got a scratch on him.' I stopped and shook my head. 'If I had put two and two together it would have been simple" That had been the answer I had in my head a hundred years ago on the Albianna. There was something wrong but I couldn't put my finger on it.

The question was what had I seen?" I continued to
the silent Granny.

"It worked out for the Russians far better than
they could have expected. Henry's parents had been
killed in the war. An aunt his only living relative
died in a bus accident. It might be interesting to
look into that to. They shoot Henry. He survives
after two months in hospital. He leaves and they nail
him, this time permanently. He was due to come
back to Britain but at that point the American
blockade of Cuba comes up. Seven other agents die.
Those guys die to make the Americans blind . Their
Henry stays on station bravely doing his job . It's
the old "this man is above reproach," confidence
game the KGB used to work. He couldn't be suspect
he has suffered the most." I laughed but it wasn't
pleasant." Those seven men died to cover the
switch. See two Dutch agents had seen
Youdonavich when he was in the Netherlands a
short time before some mastermind came up with
this fiddle.

The Dutchmen had to die because they could
identify the bogus Say. The rest were the top men in
the networks. One set of murders covering a second.

Say or Youdonavich stayed deep under cover for
thirty years. He was all over the Middle East, here,

God knows what damage he's done.' I stopped to catch my breath and to marvel at the man. 'I don't know how he did it? My nerves would have snapped years ago but then look at Philby .Anyway he had been passing information back all that time. You'd better look into that."

The second part of the troika doll was Dubois" .I continued 'He did huge damage to the Russians while he was still part of the firm. I mean, I've even heard the stories about Hungary and East Germany. So they dumped the seven murders on him. Dropped enough clues, maybe had the bogus Say back them up. Dubois was smart. He knew head office had turned on him. I think he had a pretty good idea that Philby and the others existed but couldn't prove it. He wasn't going to Lauriet House. So he skipped to New Orleans and offered his services to the Americans. They also had their doubts about our organization. Dubois has been helping them on and off for years.

Meanwhile he started to fall into this sex thing he created. The sexual information on all those powerful people. He made sure no one could touch him . The fact that we turned on him, made him very sensitive. He made up his mind it wasn't going to happen again.

The problem was that at the end he started to believe his own press. He got a god complex. Not only was he getting into international kidnapping but he was blackmailing Say. You see he had found out the truth. That's why he had Say put me on to Ti Buddy. He of course was working for Dubois.

By that point the Soviets had fallen apart. Say had to stay productive or the Russians would drop him or sell him to us. He had done too much damage to expect kind treatment. He was too old to go back to Russia. So he came up with this big new plan. He told me at our last meeting that the new cover here was for something really big. It hit me afterward that he was going to be the head source for information from the Caribbean basin or South America. We have Joes and friends all over the place, that drop bits and pieces of industrial information into our hands periodically. The Russians could profit big time if that was funneled to them. They'd finance that. So I had to die because I could mess up his little plan.

He let me and the girl in that night to see what I knew. Once he figured you had some part of it he helped me 'cause he was afraid you'd catch on."

I stopped for a moment and let it sink in.

"Is that all?"

"Well, the third part of the troika, was they had a

deep agent. After we started to find the Moles from Cambridge, they couldn't produce any more . I don't know if there are any more Say's out there..

"So you came here to kill Say." Granny coached

"Yes because he also tried to kill Breakleaf. Henry couldn't let Pimple tell us who he was. Toad was being faithful as he had been taught. Toad wouldn't have given him up just on standard grounds but Say couldn't take the chance. So he killed the warder, shot Harry and wasted good old Pimple in the bargain.

He almost got me too. I was lucky on Puerto Rico. Those three goons were his. I got two of them but Marg got the other. She's good Granny .I think she wants your job, so watch out." I heard him laugh a little.

" It started when Sasha told me that the other man on the Albianna was 'in house'. I thought I had seen Say on the ship but I thought it was a lookalike. I should have checked."

"Not very nice of you to tell him we had the card." Said Granny very peeved.

" I knew, you were going to give it back, to the Americans. Also, I never said we had it, just people behind me." I figured the chance was too good to let pass. I had nothing else to trade and I had to find out who was trying to kill me. If I made a mistake, I'll take responsibility .

The info was already in the Firm's hands for a day and had probably been used by then." Granny cleared his throat uncomfortably.

"So, he also killed the Chinese Spy as well?" Granny asked.

" Harry thinks not. Someone the Chinese sent in from Panama did Bessy the Hun." I finished.

"Just for the record I wouldn't have killed Say. I know that now. I am not God. I can't just kill people . They have to be coming at me with intent. Then it's self preservation." I meant it too.

Chapter seventeen -8:15 A.m., La Rue St. Louie,
Marigot, St. Martin, French West Indies.

Consequences

 The wind had the silky consistency of a woman's
breast. Its warm passing touched me in many ways.
Beauty was a part of the moment. It was fueled by
relief at my decision and the knowledge that Granny
would take responsibility for the next step in my
drama.

 I looked back at the tall blond spy and considered
what the possibilities might be. His linear face was
far off, like clouds over a mountain range, visible
but untouchable in their solitude. Finally, he looked
at his watch, then me.

 "How do you know it was Say who killed Jerry?"
He asked.

 "There is no way any common person or
individual who Jerry did not trust would have gotten
into that cabin. It came down to a second or so. He
hesitated then went for his gun. That meant whoever
shot him, knew the proper knock sequence, had the
door open and was acceptable to Jerry. It could have
been me' I said honestly, 'but I was in the dining
room.

Harry checked that out. Sasha told me the other man on the ship was 'in house' or a line spy for the Russians. I am sure I saw Say on the ship.

Henry said, you knew all about the kidnapping ring on St. Martin but you didn't. He said you knew that Tisani was on the island but you didn't. Until I told you.

My gut tells me it's him but then that's not very scientific. I checked, out the bullets, it was a Walther. Given its our gun of choice and the Americans have moved on to Italian made Beretta from the heavy forty-fives, it could only be one of us. Or maybe it was someone else who was using the gun to lead us off like the Chinese but to the best of my knowledge they all used Colts.

Anyway that's why you get the big bucks. I didn't kill them Granny,' I said with fatigue, 'Or do I get to play Jewel in this little fable?"

"No!" said my boss and with that he took off his straw hat and wiped his forehead with the back of his hand. I heard the scream of fear and pain knowing it was Saraphina's voice. I also knew equally well that Henry Say was no more. In the instant prior to the siren call of pain and loss from the huge black woman, who had taken care of so many of Say's needs, the resound of a solid impact from a bullet hitting the armored glass had come to me. I half stood. Granny suggested a walk down the beach. A yacht which had been hidden by the cottage and it's wall now made slow progress along the shore. It was at least forty feet long with red detailing. She now picked up speed and moved off rather quickly. The shooter had been on the yacht and Granny was here to witness or more likely trigger the execution. He had known . The bullet would have simply holed the armored glass and blown a good part of the mole away.

"I was just wondering which little hand signal had you worked out for my demise?" I ask just to bug Granny.

"Something to do with scratching my backside, if I remember correctly." He said completely nonplussed.

"Well I guess as long as it's relevant." I returned although I was close to the end of my witty repartee. I hurt now more then ached and fatigue was coming into the equation.

We walk along silently for a few minutes while the Hee! Haw! police sirens howl out from the city.

"We didn't know he was a mole.' Said Granny almost casually. 'I had him evaluating South American material as a final filter before it was

passed on to London. One of Jerry's Joes mentioned
a bit of information he had sent in, which we could
have used a great deal but never got. Jerry reported
in and started to talk to some of his other people
that I had transferred to Henry. They all started to
come up with small bits good bits that had been left
out in the condensed reports. I figured Henry had
turned. The reason was the problem we could not
work out. The why of it. Now I know. He killed
Jerry because he knew Jerry was chasing the
answer. He then placed the blame on you. Said he
had a contact on the ship who said that you had
done it." Granny stopped. " To be fair when you
went to Sasha we thought he was right. However,
you are right Harry did confirm. Also you went to
New York and saved all those people. Henry Say
wouldn't have and if you had turned, the last thing
you would do is go out after enemies exterior, given
the ones you had so close at hand.

" So you decided I was clear and had him
wasted." I said with more clarity.

"No! his death was made ready about a week ago
when Sir Mortimer signed the order. As you know
the Star Court or some judicial body always passes
on the evidence before the order is made out. I was

to see this thing through. He wanted everyone to know the government would not put up with its people being killed. I personally would have turned him or put him in Lauriet House." Granny finished. and looked out toward the sea for the small boat that would take him out to the cruiser

"I still can't figure out why Jerry went for the Chinese like that. I mean when you look at it, the Yanks will provide the information at another date and so forth. I was pleased because I really don't want the Chi-coms to have that kind of availability. They don't play nice and they have their own agenda." I said.

"Jerry or Jerold as he liked to be called, was spot on with that situation. Langley didn't know a great deal about it. Senator Tilly has had to answer for a great number of things, although he won't be arrested. I fear he will not be pulling that little bit of comedy again.

You see our Chinese friends are deeply involved with Panama. They are rebuilding the canal. Of course controlling a vital life link to the west coast of the US. The real difficulty with that sort of thing is that the Americans left a number of great thick concrete bunkers at both ends of the Canal Zone They have some from both wars."

"I wonder how many rockets they could hide in those satellite protected installations? Of course they would have problems getting the components in under the American's noses." I suggested

"Not really. Knowing the Chinese they would probably have the parts come in, secreted in plastic bags and reconstruct them on sight.' Granny's laugh was not pleasant. He then continued 'that little gambit would place them ten minutes from the American boarder by rocket. The satellite defense system would be looking out over the Pacific."

"Just as a side bar they could probably reach Western Europe where all the defenses face the Russians." I added.

"Yes, I think there should be a very different look taken at the situation from NSA and Langley. I have a feeling the problem might go away."

"It seemed Jerry earned his DSO.".

"Yes, with all his idiosyncrasy, he turned out to be a pillar. We will be want to replace him. "   I smiled and raised my hand, like a second grader.

"I think not too many people will be angry with you. It will take time for this to cool down but I have already covered off what happened with the senior Service people in the Hague and Paris so I don't think you will have any problems getting off the island.

" Someone once defined what you just did as murder with a coat of paint." I ruminated.

" It certainly puts a different perspective on the term Waste Not doesn't it?"

" I can't say if what we did was right or not."

" You had better.' Granny turned. 'You good guy, them bad guy's. Either we are right, old boy or we are wrong. However, we are all there is. So we are right and that is all. The death that comes from that truth is what dictates the right and the wrong."

"Boss why not just give it up? We could buy a boat and take rich Americans out to catch sail fish. Get them drunk and bring them back. I figure we could save the species with enough booze." Granny actually laughed it was clear and honest not horsy. I continued. 'We could bring our families down. Let our kids grow up here where there is less hate and more freedom. Maybe not teach them anything just let them sail the Caribbean and live their dreams."

Granny seemed to see his daughter running free on the beach for a moment but then his face closed in again.

"Utopia's I have found, are based on two things, money and dreams. Well we have the dreams . Do you have a great lot of loot hidden away somewhere Michael?"

" No." I shook my head to the negative.

" Then there are only two ways to obtain it. Work for it or steal it. You could of course live poor but I like my suits and telly. I have my dream already. Someday I will become head of the firm." This showed a lot of trust in me and I was gratified.

"Well, Sir Teddy I guess we could do worse." I gave him my vote of confidence.

"Thank you, however, Michael your dream has reality for you. Don't lose it. I'll see what I can do. As your children go off to school and you're really ready to retire, I'm sure we will need security people on Anquila or the Turks. I won't forget what you've done. You and your lady deserve the chance to follow your dream.' He paused for a moment 'In reality I think you'd go stark raving bonkers down here in a week.' He smiled as did . 'However I have been proven wrong before." A soft buzz came to us by the shoreward wind. It was almost dark now and the boat's arrival and departure would be hidden in its cloak."

"Boss are we winning.?" I asked before thinking.

"At the moment yes for a little bit but that will

change." Granny removes his sandals and placed his feet in the waves like a Brighten tourist. There was the little of the boy there for a moment that he had been. I said nothing as this moment was important. The waves allowed him to escape for a few precious minutes from his next big decision.

" Boss you can tell them you figured out he was a mole. I got lots of brownie points for this case and I figure it would make you look good."

" The idea was yours. You worked it out. It stays that way.' I'll obtain my Knighthood the good old fashion way."

"Grease, I'm sorry I didn't know you were related to the Queen." Granny laughed again loud and long.

"You are not the common man, you're loyal as well. Someday in the future maybe we will try your utopia. You never know, perhaps by then I'll have lost my taste for adrenaline." We both knew that wasn't going to happen, for either of us.

The boat materialized out of the mist and stopped. Granny got on board like a grand admiral and turned to me.. I took out the Luger and passed it to him handle first. "Maybe you should have this. It was Jerry's. It will make a keepsake." Granny took the silenced pistol and placed it on the bottom of the rubber dingy. I had wiped it so I didn't care what happened to it.

"We're using a lot of ancient artillery aren't we?" I ask

"Its dead hard to trace. The bores are not available." Said Granny.

"By the way, why kill Henry?"

"It would be a nasty trial and we would look stupid. The Russians would have a field day. We probaly wouldn't get a lot out of him and there's no one left to trade. Sometimes you just do the expedient thing. Mainly it's because of Jerry and Breakleaf we won't have our people killed. There was a convention in 1973. We just met it's conditions."

" Check in when you get home. " Granny waves and they were off.

Chapter eighteen - 8:30 P.m. Near Marigot, St. Martin, French West Indies

The Winds That Blow

I sit for sometime watching Granny leave. He is a dot in the mist when I get up to return to my rented Golf. The night is alive with the soft calls of birds and the sweetness of flowers. Not the sickening sweetness of Tahiti, where the entire place smells like dead flora but an uplifting and joyous smell. Darkness seems to hold no evils for me. The Golf starts immediately. I have taken the long way around to preclude any interaction with the police. I drive quietly back, as Maurice or one of his people, start a murder investigation that will lead to the perennial brick wall.

I seem more balanced with Say gone. I realize it is selfish but then that is what life is about. Survival is an object of great worth. If you are alive then the other chap is dead or incapacitated but at least not actively working toward your destruction.

Is God watching? Does he care? When you live the life I do, it is hard to accept that he is. Say is sitting in his house waiting to kill me. I wait outside to kill him. With all the beauty of a Caribbean night, we two idiots are hell bent on destruction.

Say for his future and his life. I for my life
certainly but there has to be more.

Is death the end? Do the lights go out as when you
are under sedation and you don't wake up? Is that
blackness the only thing? Does a well remembered
relative wait beside your bed or last place of resting
to say, "Hi!" We've been waiting for you. Your dad
and mum are just up the way a little, follow the
light." Does the joy of that meeting dissipate the
loss of the life around you, the clouds you'll never
see again the happy faces and loved ones that will
never touch you? Will the bitter remembrances of
lost struggles remain? 'Perchance to dream and
there is the rub'.

I do not know and do not want to. I wonder if
across the black boarders of death, those who you
have wronged await to pounce on your poor soul
and do it great injury. I would like to believe that
the truly evil suffer that fate, Hitler say, Attila the
Hun and so on. Of course not me. Not secure in his
blanket of brave rightfulness me.

How much more was Tisani or Say not fighting
for their nation, their right? Was God on their
side? Where would the balance be in the end? More
frightening still, say the real God was Jewish or
Buddhist. Wouldn't a lot of people get a hell of a
surprise then?

I was getting maudlin and of course I hurt a great deal. The answer, of course, you couldn't do anything about death. So until it happened you had a little time to live. Do it.

I slowly enter my hotel room and lie down. I have two or three pain pills and sleep the night through.

The Bahamas are a fan of islands, that cool the Florida coast. Nassau is a pinprick in the royal blue but soon it becomes a town of pink houses and horse drawn luxury. This befits the last stop on the Albianna's voyage around the Eastern Caribbean. I step down from the horse drawn taxi at the gang way and enter. There is consternation on the part of the Italian officers. The Captain and I have a short talk. It is not pleasant. He is disturbed by the mess and its clean up. The bullet hole in the door also disturbs him. Cherie-Lee it seems is above reproach but I am not, having disappeared before the captain and his people can discuss the matter with me.

I suggest amiably that I have spent the last four days getting this all straightened out with the British authorities. Tonight will find me available to any discussion they wish to have. As long as it is in the bright sunshine and accompanied with drinks in a civilized manner. After all one of my models was kidnapped, even with their excellent security on the ship. While a law suit was not the direction my company wished to go in, if the shoot was not complete, a substantial amount of money was at stake and should be considered. This brought an abrupt halt to the proceedings and I was sent along my way with a truce in place . No more uncomfortable questions and no more talk of lawyers, it was too nice a day. I bow myself out gracefully.

On the Athens deck all is quiet. Almost everyone is ashore, the rest are sprawled out on deck or getting ready to leave tomorrow, on our return trip to the United States. I trot along to Cherie's new room number and am faced by Ron, Misty's companion come security person. Ron is about six two and solid muscle. He may look stupid but the blockish empty look, hides an excellent brain. I have had long conversations with him about International Socialism and so on.

Today he is the guard by the gate. I ask politely to enter and am asked politely to wait. He goes in and I hear a light conversation between Cherie-Lee and a male voice which I take to be Don her husband.

I haven't done anything, so steeled in that truth, I

enter when given the high sign, by the big man. Don got up to shake hands. Cherie sits bedraggled, in an untidy heap. Her freckles are all visible and I fear so are at least three nights of sleep loss.

She looks up and there are tears.

"Where did you go McFurson, you creep, you disappeared when I needed you. Her face pouched and then she cried deep. I sat beside her ignoring Don's malevolent stare.

"Cherie I had to stay behind and clear up the mess. I filled out more paper then you could imagine. I couldn't have this in the media or everyone from Vogue on down would be waiting to pounce. Which would be fine for marketing but I was worried about you." I soothed.

" That terrible old woman she wanted to know about you and she seemed to think you were some kind of secret agent or something." Oh! Good now I have to lie my ass off. Well here goes.

" What happened exactly?" I asked to confirm what she knew. Never give out more information then you really have to. Lies are progressive so leave as little as possible to chance.

" They stripped me naked and searched me like I was already dead. Then they asked about some post card and when I couldn't answer they got me to write a note. I wouldn't so they said they'd kill me.

I didn't want to die, so I wrote it. Did I do wrong?"
She said through her tears.

" No!" I said hugging her, ignoring old Don. This
was my fault so I would take care of it.

"Listen these people figured they could kidnap you
and get the money right on board ship. Have me
transfer it into a bank account in Switzerland or
something. At least that's what the British Police
said. I figure they had you write to me because I am
kind of in charge. They would have done better with
Nome but it was me. I don't know about you being
naked but when I stopped that guy in the hallway he
had you over his arm. You looked like you were
pretty doped up. I asked to get you back and he
turned you over after I started yelling. He made a
run for it. I got you to Nome and got a doctor, then
I had the guy arrested. The old lady and the other
two were arrested because they sweated it out of
the first one. They are all in jail now . I guess the
British had other things to talk to them about . You
know cops they don't tell you much. I missed the
ship so they made me give them information on
everyone else and then I was allowed to meet you
here."

Cherie's eyes said I was full of it. I had lost a
friend

and perhaps I deserved it but it hurt all the same. I never thought back on that windy warm day when we made hot dogs this would happen. At least I had kept her alive.

" Is that all?" She asked.

"Yes everything." I said lying through my teeth.

"Fine, I'd like to be alone if you wouldn't mind." Cherie would keep our secret or secrets. However, I would no longer be her friend and would no longer bask in her glory. I give up a great deal for Queen and country this was probably the worst. At least Don was back and he would help her.

Nome on the other hand knew me too well. The shoot and layout was completed as per my instructions. I could expect no less of Nome. Of course, he wanted to get paid too. He looked at me and asked the same hard question. What was I? He knew it wasn't purely security and he knew about the bullet hole. I said I didn't know anything about it. He smiled but it wasn't very pleasant. I had a feeling it would be a while before I worked with him again. There would always be the story of my background and a bullet hole in a door to pass around. In some cases it would make me more popular. In others it would make buyers more reticent. In the end there were lots of other customers out there and my reputation did not stand on this one point in time. It being a long and productive one would make the customers I had stay and others come back.

I return home once more by many different loops and directions. At the house my wife looks at the wounds and makes love straddling me although she does not like the position as it makes her work more but in the end we enjoy each other. She lays out on my shoulder and sleeps. I allow my body to relax and overcome the pain in my chest and ribs.

The darkened room is a fortress against the outside world which has now entered my narrow boundaries. I will have to be very selective about assignments from now on so that I can return to this little place of security.

It is strange how important small things being in place calm the mind. The Dalton lady on my wives bureau. My model of the 1970 MGGT the first car I ever owned, hold the spirit and life that was and is in the room. They the permanent things of my fortress allow me to sleep in peace.

I am trapped by my own actions, by the promise I have made. I was a part of a murder, it was my witness that killed Say. I must live with this. I cannot make a judgement on Granny or Mortimer. They are governed by different rules and I have no say in them. I must be the pawn or leave the table.

All I ever wanted to do was the right thing. That was once simple. I had played Sir Galihad and was

paying for it. Would I have done it any different?
No.

As Henry Say said 'We are the last line of defense
for the golden towers of the West.' This small room
with the smells of our love making is part of that
protected place. How long can it remain?

Perhaps we will create a machine that will make
all men equally happy, well and fed. Until that day
we will do what is necessary to keep the walls
defended and the towers standing.

End It

McFurson Will Return In Want Not.

This novel is pure fiction. The characters
do not exist. The situations are strictly for
the amusement of the reader, these events
have no substance in reality and have
never happened.
While locations do exist they are only
backdrops. Any references to persons
living or dead and any likeness to those
persons is strictly coincidental.

Thank you for reading my book.
George V. Henderson

COVET NOT
GEORGE V. HENDERSON

SPY NOT
GEORGE V. HENDERSON

WASTE NOT

georgev_henderson@hotmail.com